VEIL OF FORGOTTEN MEMORIES

T. S. VEIL

Made with ♥ on the Notion Press Platform
www.notionpress.com

To the victims and their families who lost their loved ones
during the Wayanad landslides,

This story is a tribute to your resilience, courage, and the
enduring strength of the human spirit. May the memories
of those who were lost continue to live on in our hearts,
and may their stories be remembered always.

With deepest respect and sorrow,

Contents

Author's Note

Veil of Forgotten Memories is a work of fiction inspired by the tragic Wayanad landslides, which left a lasting impact on the lives of those affected. While this story draws upon the resilience and strength of the community that endured this disaster, all characters, events, and scenarios depicted in this book are purely products of imagination. Any resemblance to real persons, living or deceased, or to actual events, is entirely coincidental. The narrative has been crafted with the utmost respect for the victims of the landslide and their families, with the intention of honoring their memories and acknowledging the profound pain and loss they experienced. This story serves as a tribute to their courage and the enduring spirit of the human heart in the face of unimaginable tragedy.

As a writer, I strive to create original and engaging stories. However, I recognize that storytelling is a vast and shared landscape, and it is possible that some plot elements, themes, or ideas in this book may bear resemblance to other works. Any such similarities are entirely coincidental and unintentional. This story is the product of my imagination, and any overlap with existing works is purely coincidental and not a result of copying or imitating.

Foreword

The story you are about to read is rooted in the rich, vibrant, yet often tumultuous land of Wayanad, where the echoes of history and nature's fury intertwine. Inspired by the tragic landslides of 2024, *Veil of Forgotten Memories* is more than just a tale of suspense and the supernatural—it's a reflection on the resilience of the human spirit and the silent witnesses that landscapes often become to the stories of those who inhabit them.

In crafting this narrative, I sought to explore the delicate balance between life and death, the seen and the unseen, and the ways in which the past continues to shape our present. This book is a blend of fiction and reality, where the supernatural serves as a metaphor for the unresolved grief, loss, and the mysteries that linger in the wake of disaster.

While the characters and events in this story are products of imagination, they are woven with threads of truth, representing the countless lives affected by the Wayanad landslides. The land itself becomes a character in this story, a silent keeper of memories, both tragic and hopeful.

I hope this story resonates with you, drawing you into a world where the past refuses to be forgotten, and where every memory, no matter how painful, has a place in the tapestry of life. As you journey with Aadhira, Dev, and the other characters, may you find in their struggles and triumphs a reflection of the enduring human spirit.

Thank you for choosing to embark on this journey with me.

PREFACE

In the heart of Wayanad, where lush greenery contrasts with the scars of its past, *Veil of Forgotten Memories* draws inspiration from the 2024 landslides that reshaped lives and landscapes. This novel explores the impact of such a tragedy on both the physical world and the human spirit, revealing how loss and resilience intertwine.

While a work of fiction, the story is deeply rooted in the realities of grief and the search for justice. Through Aadhira's journey, we confront the unspoken pain and unanswered questions that follow disaster, paying tribute to those lost and the injustices that persist.

Writing this book has been a way to honor the memories of those who perished and to highlight the enduring human spirit. Each character and plot twist reflects real struggles and the quest for peace.

I hope this story not only captivates you but also resonates with a deeper truth: that in even the darkest times, the pursuit of truth and remembrance can lead to healing. Thank you for joining me on this journey.

Acknowledgements

Writing *Veil of Forgotten Memories* has been a deeply personal and rewarding journey, and I am profoundly grateful to those who have supported me along the way. To the families and communities affected by the Wayanad landslides, your strength and resilience inspired this story and gave it purpose. I extend my heartfelt thanks to the friends, mentors, and readers who provided invaluable encouragement and feedback. A special thank you to the professionals and experts who contributed their insights, helping to ground the narrative in authenticity. Your support has made this book not just a work of fiction, but a tribute to real lives and real struggles.

Prologue

On the night of July 30, 2024, the serene villages of Wayanad, Kerala, were devastated by a series of catastrophic landslides. At around 2 a.m., torrents of mud, boulders, and uprooted trees engulfed the villages, burying homes and trapping residents in a merciless deluge.

The initial landslide struck while villagers were asleep, leading to frantic cries for help and heart-wrenching phone calls from those trapped beneath debris. The destruction was extensive: entire villages, including Mundakkai, Chooralmala, Attamala, and Noolpuzha, were swept away, along with roads, bridges, and plantations. The lush landscape was left barren and desolate.

As dawn broke, the scale of the disaster became clear. With at least 392 confirmed dead and 150 missing, the loss was staggering. Hundreds more were injured as rescue efforts, hindered by ongoing rain and the extent of the damage, struggled to reach survivors. The Indian Air Force, NDRF, army, and local teams worked tirelessly, but hope waned with each passing hour.

The aftermath revealed a land haunted by the memories of those lost, with villages in ruins and communities forever changed. The tragedy had not only claimed lives but also disrupted the sense of security and belonging in these communities. As the nation mourned and recovery efforts began, the people of Wayanad faced the daunting task of rebuilding their lives amidst the enduring scars of this catastrophic event.

I

The Arrival

Five years. It's been five years since the landslide of 2024 ripped through Wayanad, tearing the earth apart, swallowing everything in its path. I remember how the hills were once so alive, draped in green, bursting with life. Now, it's all gone—replaced by a barren, scarred wasteland. The jagged lines of destruction cut through the terrain, a permanent reminder of where the earth gave way, swallowing trees, homes, and too many lives to count.

Walking through what remains is like stepping into a graveyard. The remnants of homes—broken bricks, rusted beams, and crumbling foundations—jut out of the ground like tombstones, telling the silent story of a tragedy that wiped out entire communities. There's nothing left but silence, an eerie, heavy silence, only broken by the occasional gust of wind. That wind, though—it doesn't just blow through. It howls like its mourning, singing a song for the lives lost.

But even in places like this, there's always someone watching, waiting. The desolation didn't scare off the Verma Development Corporation. No, they saw the opportunity. Ravi Verma, the man behind the company, always had an eye for turning the forgotten into something shiny and new. He did it in Mumbai, transforming empty fields into suburbs. He did it again in Chennai, turning dry, dead land into a tech hub. And now, he's set his sights on Wayanad—this cursed land that everyone else had abandoned. But not Verma. He sees something the rest of us don't.

The project Verma had in mind wasn't just ambitious—it was downright audacious. He imagined a sleek, modern residential complex rising defiantly from the wreckage, almost taunting the memories of what came before. In his mind's eye, it was perfect: a tight-knit community complete with high-end amenities, contemporary homes, manicured parks, and a bustling commercial hub. He saw it as a beacon—a sign that progress could outshine tragedy, that renewal was possible, even here, where the land still seemed to grieve.

When the machines arrived, they shattered the silence like an alarm clock after a nightmare. The bulldozers tore into the earth, erasing what was left of the old world to make room for Verma's new one. Piece by piece, they ripped away the scars of the past—the rocks, the twisted trees, even the fragments of homes. Everything was swept aside, crushed, or buried beneath the steel and concrete of what would be the foundation of this new, gleaming future.

But the past doesn't stay buried so easily. As the crews worked, they would occasionally hit something more than just rock and dirt. A broken piece of pottery, an ancient tool, sometimes even bones—the skeletal remains of lives lost to that relentless landslide. Every discovery whispered of the people who had lived here, who had been swallowed by the disaster. But those whispers were quickly silenced.

The relics were cataloged, then forgotten. The focus was always on what was coming, on the future Verma promised, the new life he envisioned for the land and the people who would one day call it home.

Day by day, I watched Verma's dream rise from the ground. The sleek apartment buildings dominated the skyline, modern homes taking shape beneath the relentless Kerala sun. Wide, tree-lined streets stretched out, connecting everything like the veins of a community that didn't exist yet—but soon would. Fresh coats of paint gleamed in the daylight, signaling a new beginning. Verma, ever the perfectionist, was there constantly, his sharp eyes missing nothing. If a line was off, if the grass wasn't perfectly aligned with his plans, he'd make sure it was fixed. This was his masterpiece, and nothing short of flawless would do.

But what Verma couldn't see, what no one seemed to notice, was the land itself. Beneath the concrete and steel, something lingered. The earth had been forced into submission, yes, but it hadn't forgotten. The hum of construction couldn't fully drown out the silence of the past. That silence—beneath the machinery, beneath the new streets—carried stories, stories buried so deep they hadn't surfaced yet. But the land remembered. And it wasn't done with its secrets.

When I first arrived, the place was buzzing with excitement, the kind that comes with new beginnings. The first few residents, including me, were trickling in, eager to start over. For me, it was an escape—a chance to leave the weight of the past behind. That's what this place promised: renewal, a fresh start. But the moment I stepped out of my car, something felt... off. A chill hung in the air, sticking to me like a shadow I couldn't shake.

The road leading into the complex was pristine, freshly paved and lined with delicate saplings, their potential shelter still years away. The scent of fresh paint filled the air, mixing with the sounds of life in progress. Workers were adding final touches, neighbors greeted each other as they settled into their new homes, and I could hear the distant laughter of kids testing out the playground for the first time.

On the surface, everything seemed perfect—shiny, new. But something beneath all that felt wrong. The homes were modern, with enormous windows designed to let in light, the park teemed with activity, and the fountain in the middle bubbled serenely. Yet, just beyond the edges of it all stood the forest, dark and ancient, untouched by all the progress happening around it. Those trees—silent and imposing—watched everything with a kind of stillness that felt older than the scars of the land.

As I made my way to my apartment, excitement battled with something else—something colder, more insidious. There was a weight in the air, a heaviness that clung to the walls of my new place. The fresh paint couldn't mask it. I stood at the window, looking out at the hills in the distance, their jagged lines still visible, a stark reminder of the devastation that had once torn this place apart.

Then night fell. In the fading light, the complex, once vibrant and alive, becomes dulled. The sounds of life quieted, replaced by an unsettling silence that settled over everything. The trees at the forest's edge seemed to loom closer, their dark silhouettes like sentinels guarding something they weren't willing to reveal. Beneath my feet, the ground felt less solid, as if it was only a thin veil covering something deeper, something waiting.

That's when I felt it. Something old, something ancient, was stirring. It had been lying dormant, but it wasn't asleep anymore. This wasn't just land—this place was alive with the past, a past that clung to the present, refusing to be forgotten. And those whispers I'd tried to ignore? They were growing louder, more insistent. They weren't just in my head anymore. I was being watched. Drawn in. Pulled toward something that had been waiting for me long before I ever set foot here.

The air in the room thickened, almost buzzing with energy. It wasn't just memories of the past—it was more than that. And suddenly, I understood. This place had chosen me. Whatever was buried here, whatever was haunting this land, it wasn't done with me. My journey wasn't over. In fact, it had only just begun.

II

Aadhira

I guess I should start by telling you who I am, right? My name's Aadhira. I was born in the late '90s, in this tiny village tucked away deep in the forests of Kerala. You probably haven't heard of it—it's that kind of place, hidden from the world, where life moves at its own slow rhythm. My family? Well, they were about as traditional as they come. We lived the kind of life that didn't stray far from what was expected. Change wasn't exactly welcome, and anything that didn't fit into the neat little box of "normal" was met with suspicion.

But me? I never quite fit into that box. Even when I was little, I could feel things, sense things that no one else seemed to notice. It's hard to explain, but it's like the air would shift around me, or I'd hear these whispers that weren't really there—or at least not for anyone else. And something... unseen, like there were forces moving just out of sight, always lingering in the background. I couldn't always make sense of it, but I knew it was real. I knew I was different.

I learned early on not to talk about it too much. You can imagine how well that went over in a village where tradition ruled. My family, my neighbors—they didn't understand. Hell, sometimes I didn't understand. But it was there, a part of me I couldn't ignore, no matter how hard I tried.

And that's how it all started, really. The rest? Well, that's a story that's still unfolding, isn't it?

When I was seven, I used to spend a lot of time by the riverbank. It was my escape; you know? A place where I didn't have to deal with the noise of the village, the constant expectations, the watchful eyes. There, it was just me and the water, the rustling of the trees, the hum of nature. But there was this one evening—one I'll never forget. Dusk had settled in, and the forest had fallen silent in a way that wasn't normal. It wasn't peaceful—it was heavy, almost like the air itself was holding its breath.

As the sun sank lower, casting these long shadows over the water, I felt something strange, like a pull, right from the earth beneath my feet. The usual sounds—birds, wind, the river's steady flow—had all vanished, replaced by this stillness that was... charged. It wasn't just quiet; it was like the entire world had shifted without me noticing.

Then, I heard it. Or felt it, I'm not even sure. A whisper, faint, more of an echo than a voice, creeping through the silence. My heart was pounding, and there was this sorrow in the air—something deep, something ancient. It wasn't coming from anywhere I could see, but I knew it was there. I could feel it, pressing down on me, filling the surrounding air. Suddenly, the river felt alive in a way it hadn't before, my sanctuary. The water seemed to pulse, like it had its own heartbeat, matching mine. The surrounding colors grew more intense, almost unreal.

That's when it hit me: these weren't voices of the living. They were spirits. They had found me, somehow drawn to me because of this thing inside me, this connection I didn't fully understand yet. And the strangest part? I wasn't afraid, not really. The fear melted away into something else—understanding. The spirits weren't there to hurt me. They had found me because I could hear them. I could feel them. And in that moment, I knew my life would never be the same.

When the night finally wrapped around me, the voices faded. But I was different. I felt like I carried something new, something heavy but undeniable. That night marked the beginning of something—a journey I didn't ask for, but one I knew I was tied to now, whether or not I wanted it.

I went back home, terrified, but changed. That experience—it left a mark on me that never faded. As I got older, my abilities grew stronger. I could feel other people's emotions like they were my own, sense spirits, sometimes even catch glimpses of the past, like memories that weren't mine. What had once been my escape became a burden, especially as the village noticed. They didn't understand, didn't want to understand. To them, what I had wasn't a gift. It was unnatural. Dangerous, even. And so the surrounding whispers grew, only this time they weren't from the spirits—they were from the people I'd grown up with.

One night, I was ripped from sleep by a dream so terrifying it felt like it had sunk claws into my very soul. I woke up, my heart pounding in my chest, skin drenched in cold sweat, and the images still clinging to me like they were too real to shake off. In the dream, I was standing on that dusty road leading through our village, bathed in the low, eerie light of a setting sun. Everything around me—the houses, the trees—looked familiar, but the air felt heavy with something ominous, something waiting to happen.

Then I heard it. A distant rumble that grew louder and more menacing. When I turned, I saw a bullock cart racing down the road—far too fast, the bullocks wild-eyed, frothing at the mouth as if possessed by some unseen terror. The cart was piled high with sugarcane, wobbling dangerously, and every instinct in me screamed that this wasn't just an accident waiting to happen. It was a disaster barreling toward us. And then I saw where it was headed: Mr. Narayanan's house, right at the end of the road. He was standing outside, completely unaware of the death rushing straight for him.

I tried to scream. Tried to move. But I couldn't. My body refused to listen. All I could do was watch in helpless horror as the cart veered off, crashing into his house. The sound of splintering wood, the terrified screams of his family, and the sickening thud as Mr. Narayanan's body hit the ground echoed in my mind. It was so vivid, so real, like I was living it.

When I woke up, shaking, I knew—this wasn't just a dream. It was a warning, a vision. Something was going to happen, and it was going to happen soon.

I ran straight to my parents, still breathless from the nightmare. "Amma, Appa," I gasped, "I saw it! A bullock cart—it's going to crash into Narayanan Uncle's house. We need to warn him!"

My mother looked at me, her face soft with concern but worn with the familiar weight of dismissing my fears. "Aadhira, it was just a dream. Dreams mean nothing."

"No!" I cried, grabbing her hand, desperate for her to understand. "This wasn't just a dream. It's real, Amma. I felt it. We have to do something!"

My father, ever the practical one, rested a hand on my shoulder. "You've always had an imagination, Aadhira. But it's just that—imagination. Don't worry yourself over it."

Their refusal to believe me felt like a punch to the gut. I was powerless to make them see what I knew was coming. But I couldn't just stand by and let it happen. I ran to Mr. Narayanan's house, hoping, praying, that I could stop it.

When I got there, I found him in the front yard, just like in my dream, tending to his bullocks. I ran up to him, breathless, pleading. "Uncle, please, listen to me! I had a dream—a vision—a cart is going to crash into your house. Please, stay away from the road!"

He chuckled softly, like I was telling him some harmless childhood tale. "You have quite the imagination, little one. There's nothing to worry about. Dreams are just dreams."

"No, Uncle," I begged, my voice cracking with the weight of the fear I couldn't shake. "Please, just be careful, for your family's sake."

He smiled kindly at me, his eyes full of the same gentle disbelief as my parents'. "Go home now, Aadhira. There's nothing to fear."

And so I did. I went home, defeated, praying with every fiber of my being that my vision wouldn't come true.

But the next day, the village was torn apart by screams and chaos. The bullock cart had careened out of control, just like I had seen in my dream, crashing into Mr. Narayanan's house. And just like in the vision, Mr. Narayanan was killed instantly.

The nightmare had become reality, and I was powerless to stop it.

The news of the accident spread like wildfire, but instead of thanking me for trying to warn them, the village turned on me. They didn't see me as someone who tried to help.

No, they saw me as the cause. The whispers that had always followed me grew louder—now I wasn't just strange; I was cursed. A witch, they called me, the one who brought this tragedy upon them. Doors that had once opened to welcome me were slammed in my face. Children I'd grown up with were pulled away from me, their parents telling them not to speak my name.

Our family, once respected, was now treated like we carried a plague. People avoided us on the street, and when they talked about us, it was in fearful whispers, as if even mentioning my name might summon disaster. I became a ghost in my village, haunted by the very people I'd known all my life. My abilities, which I had always struggled to understand, weren't seen as gifts anymore. To them, I had unleashed something dark, something they couldn't forgive.

I pulled away from it all. What else could I do? I turned inward, finding refuge in a world that made sense, a world I could control—computers. Cybersecurity became my escape. The logic, the predictability of it all, was something I could cling to. And with time, my intuition, the very thing that had caused so much pain, actually made me a better analyst. By the time I reached my mid-twenties, I had secured a remote job and saved enough to finally leave the village behind for good.

When I first heard about the new housing complex in Wayanad, it felt like a sign. A fresh start, far away from the ghosts of my past. I could live there. No one would know who I was, no one would care. It was a chance to build a life without the weight of everything that had happened hanging over me.

But Wayanad... Wayanad had its own secrets. The moment I moved in, I felt it—something familiar, something unsettling. That same energy I'd felt all those years ago when the spirits first found me by the riverbank. I'd worked so hard to push it down, to bury it, but it didn't stay quiet for long. The whispers returned. Louder. More insistent. It wasn't just the odd flicker of lights or the sudden cold drafts that unsettled me. It was the feeling, deep in my bones, that I wasn't alone. That I was being watched, drawn into something bigger than I realized.

I soon understood that I hadn't chosen this place. It had chosen me. The land, with its dark, tangled history, was reaching out, calling for something—justice, maybe, or simply to be heard. And it had found me, the one person who couldn't escape the whispers, who couldn't turn a blind eye to the things others refused to see.

The hauntings, the strange occurrences—they weren't random. They were signs. Clues. And my so-called curse? It was the key to unlocking the truth buried beneath the surface of this place. As I dug into the history of the land, the housing society, I uncovered something far darker than I could have imagined—corruption, greed, and the forgotten spirits trapped within the soil.

This wasn't the fresh start I'd hoped for. It was something far more dangerous, something that tied my fate to Wayanad's dark past. My journey, I realized, wasn't about escaping. It was about confronting the very darkness I'd been running from. The land had called me here for a reason. And this time, I couldn't turn away.

III

The First Signs

Settling into this new place, I tried to lean into the excitement of a fresh start. It wasn't easy—there was always a part of me that carried the weight of what I'd left behind—but the empty rooms, bathed in the soft glow of freshly painted walls, seemed to whisper promises of peace. Sunlight poured in through the large windows, casting everything in this warm, golden light, and for a moment, I let myself believe it. That maybe, just maybe, this was the sanctuary I'd been searching for. A place far away from the whispers of the past, where I could finally breathe.

I threw myself into making this house feel like mine. It was more than just filling the space with furniture—it was about claiming it, turning it into something that reflected me, not the shadows that had followed me for so long. The rooms, once so silent and empty, shifted, taking on a life of their own.

The oak table I'd brought from the village—it wasn't just furniture. It was a piece of my history. Its surface, worn from years of use, had seen too many shared meals, too many whispered conversations to leave behind. I placed it in the dining room, where it felt right, like it belonged. And that armchair, soft and overstuffed, the one I always curled up in with a book or just to watch the world go by—it found its place too, right by the window. The afternoon sun hit it just perfectly, filling the space with a warm, amber light. It felt like home, or at least, it was starting to.

I wanted to savor it, to hold on to this feeling of newness, of possibility. Maybe this time, I told myself, things would be different.

Hanging the curtains became more than just a chore—it was a kind of ritual for me, almost meditative. Each fabric I chose felt like a decision about how I wanted to shape this new life. I picked soft creams that calmed the eye, deep burgundies that added warmth and richness, and forest greens that echoed the wildness of Wayanad just outside my door. As I draped them over the broad windows, I could see them catching the light just right, framing not only the view but the memories I was yet to create. Each window became a portal, not just to the outside world, but to the future I was building.

In the evenings, once the sun dipped low, and the house was bathed in that soft, golden glow of the golden hour, I'd settle into the living room, finally allowing the day's exhaustion to melt away. I'd sink into my favorite chair—the one by the window—and cradle a steaming cup of tea in my hands, the fragrant steam rising to meet the lingering scent of fresh paint and new linens. It was peaceful, the silence that held promise rather than loneliness.

And there, in that moment, I'd let my mind drift. I'd imagine the life I wanted to build, the memories I hoped to fill this house with. This place wasn't just four walls and a roof; it was a canvas, and I was ready to paint my future on it, one brushstroke at a time.

But then, as the days blurred into weeks, little things shifted. At first, they were so subtle I almost didn't notice. A chill would creep through the air despite the sunlight pouring through the windows, the kind that made you wrap your arms around yourself even though you weren't cold. The floorboards would creak faintly, though I was sure I was alone. And then there were the shadows—just at the edges of my vision, flickering like something was moving there, just out of sight. I brushed it off at first, telling myself it was all just part of getting used to a new house. Every place has its quirks, right?

But soon, those small oddities chipped away at my peace. One morning, I walked into the kitchen and found everything in disarray. Utensils scattered across the counters. A coffee mug—one I had placed neatly by the sink the night before—lay shattered on the floor. I tried to convince myself it was nothing. Maybe I'd been careless, maybe I'd bumped into something in my sleep-deprived state and hadn't noticed. But deep down, I knew it didn't add up.

And it didn't stop there. Little things like this—minor disturbances that shouldn't have been happening—kept creeping in. Each time, it felt less like I was forgetting or imagining things, and more like something was happening, something I couldn't explain. The house, the peace I'd been trying to create, felt... wrong. The unease slowly settled in, and as much as I tried to rationalize it, that quiet dread crept under my skin, growing harder and harder to ignore.

It wasn't just the things I could see or touch; it was the whispers, too. They seemed to drift in and out with the wind, slipping through the walls like ghosts, just barely there—faint, disembodied murmurs that tugged at the edges of my consciousness. I've always been sensitive to these kinds of things, but here, in this house, the whispers felt amplified, more insistent, like the very structure was alive, trying to tell me something, holding onto secrets it wasn't ready to reveal.

Then came the night I heard the music.

After a long, exhausting day, I slipped into bed, grateful for the cool sheets against my skin. The room was soaked in twilight, the last traces of daylight filtering softly through the curtains. I closed my eyes, prepared to let go and finally surrender to sleep. But just as I drifted, it happened—a sound, soft at first, then unmistakable. A melody, faint and mournful, like it had been carried on the wind from another time.

My eyes flew open, heart pounding in my chest. I froze, listening. The music was barely there, delicate, like it could dissolve at any moment. But it wasn't just sound—it was emotion, pulling at me with an overwhelming sense of sorrow, longing, and something else I couldn't place. It felt old, as if it didn't belong to this world, and yet... something about it felt strangely familiar.

I sat up, adrenaline buzzing in my veins, sharpening every sense. That melody—it was unlike anything I'd ever heard before. I glanced around the room, half-expecting to see the source, to see something, but there was nothing. Everything looked the same. And yet, the air around me felt different, thick with an energy that made the hairs on the back of my neck rise.

I couldn't ignore it. Compelled by a mix of fear and curiosity, I slid out of bed, my bare feet pressing into the cool floor. The music—it called to me, even as it seemed to pull away. I followed it cautiously through the house. Each room was draped in shadows, familiar yet suddenly foreign.

The melody lingered, always just out of reach, drawing me deeper—into the living room, the kitchen, even the small study where I'd spent hours organizing my thoughts. But every time I entered a room, the music vanished, replaced by a suffocating silence that weighed on me like a stone.

I stood there, heart still racing, surrounded by darkness, the house holding its breath. It felt as though whatever had been playing that haunting tune was watching me, just beyond the edge of my sight.

My mind raced, scrambling to make sense of it. Could it have been a neighbor, maybe someone playing music late at night? But no. The melody had been too close, too... intimate. It wasn't just a tune drifting in from outside—it felt like it had been crafted for me, like it carried a message meant for my ears alone. But why? And who, or what, could send something so hauntingly beautiful and filled with such sorrow?

The house, which had once felt like a refuge, now seemed different. Darker. The corners of the rooms felt like they were stretching, the shadows growing deeper, as if they were hiding something just beyond the edge of my sight. As I wandered through the halls, I couldn't shake the feeling that I wasn't alone. The melody... it wasn't just a song. It felt like a message, or maybe even a warning. Was someone—or something—trying to reach me? Trying to tell me something that had been buried within these walls?

By the time I made it back to my bedroom, the music had faded into a barely perceptible whisper, almost like a memory that was slipping away. I stood in the doorway, frozen, listening to the silence that had replaced it. The room was quiet again, too quiet. I climbed back into bed, staring up at the ceiling, my thoughts swirling with questions I couldn't answer. What did it mean? Why had that tune found its way to me? And what was it trying to tell me?

The unease wouldn't leave me. Throughout the day, I spent more time walking through the house, stopping in corners, and standing still, listening. I was trying to catch something—anything—that could explain the strange disturbances. I even started reaching out to my neighbors, hoping to hear a story, a rumor, some kind of clue that might make sense of it all. But all I got were polite smiles, vague reassurances about the house "settling." The empty words people say when they don't really want to think about something deeper.

None of it helped. The melody, the whispers, the shadows—they weren't going away. And neither was the feeling that something, or someone, was trying to reach out to me, pulling me closer to a truth I wasn't sure I wanted to uncover.

No matter how hard I tried to convince myself that everything happening around me was just my mind playing tricks, I couldn't shake the growing certainty that this house carried more than just echoes of its past. The land it sat on may have been reshaped into a shiny, modern housing society, but something about it still bore the weight of history—an old, persistent history that refused to stay buried, whispering through the walls, creeping into every corner.

As the nights stretched longer and the shadows seemed to swallow more of the light, I found myself caught in a tug-of-war between denial and the unsettling reality forming around me. I wanted to believe it was all in my head—just exhaustion, an overactive imagination. But I couldn't ignore the feeling that I was being watched, the strange events unfolding in front of me, and the relentless, almost desperate whispers that seemed to call my name in the silence.

This house, the one I had hoped would be a place of peace, now felt like it was cocooning me in a web I didn't fully understand. And I wasn't sure I wanted to. But one thing was becoming clear—I couldn't keep ignoring it. Whatever was happening here would not go away on its own, and I had to face it, no matter how much fear clawed at the edges of my mind.

I resolved to confront whatever was lurking within these walls. The same sense of adventure that had pulled me to Wayanad in the first place now felt tainted, laced with an undercurrent of dread that I couldn't ignore. What I didn't realize was how deep this mystery went, how it tied not just to the house but to the land itself—the land that cradled secrets as old as the thick forests that embraced the hills. Secrets that wouldn't just haunt my nights, but would shake me to my core, unraveling everything I thought I knew about this place—and myself.

℘

The cool evening breeze brushed lightly against my skin as I stood on the balcony, staring out at the barren hills in the distance. They loomed there, like forgotten sentinels, stripped of life, watching silently over the scarred land. The landscape, once vibrant and full of greenery, now stretched out like a desolate tapestry unraveling in the dimming light. Those hills, even from a distance, pulled at me—an eerie allure wrapped in emptiness. They weren't just hills; they were graveyards, still bearing the wounds of the catastrophic landslide that had taken so many lives, over 392, in just one terrible day. There was something about them, something that stirred deep inside me, a primal unease that gnawed at the edges of my thoughts.

As I stood there, my mind drifted back to the stories I'd heard about that day. Stories about the torrential rains, the homes swallowed whole; the families lost to the earth. The official accounts painted the event in cold, clinical terms. They talked about how 572 millimeters of rain had fallen in just 48 hours, more than twice what had been expected. They spoke about climate change, how it had intensified the downpour, triggering the landslides that turned those hills into a monstrous force, swallowing everything in its path. Those reports laid out the facts, the numbers, the timeline. But none of that captured the actual weight of what happened here.

It wasn't just about the rain, the mud, or the destruction. There was a lingering essence, something woven into the very soil, something that refused to fade. This place held a tragedy far deeper than any statistic could convey. And as I stood there, staring at those distant hills, I couldn't shake the feeling that the land itself remembered—that the earth carried the weight of those lost lives, that the stories it held weren't finished.

I stood there, completely still, my gaze locked on the barren hills. But it wasn't just me staring at them anymore—something deeper was happening. It felt as if I were no longer separate from the landscape, as if the earth and I were connected, intertwined. The jagged ridges, the scarred valleys—they whispered to me, their voices carrying stories that had been buried long before the housing complex or the bulldozers ever arrived. I could almost see the land as it once was—pure, untouched, and teeming with life. Now, all that remained was a graveyard, a desolate stretch of broken dreams and lost lives. To anyone else, that might have been all they saw, but not to me.

To me, the hills were alive with memory. They hummed with a quiet, latent energy, as though the ground itself vibrated with the weight of the past. The further I stared, the more I could feel it—a pulse, a subtle rhythm beneath the surface. It was as if the land was trying to speak, to show me something long forgotten, something hidden beneath the ruins and scars. And I realized, in that moment, that it wasn't just a feeling. It was a call—a pull I couldn't ignore, no matter how much I might want to.

I had always been attuned to things others couldn't see—the shifts in energy, the whispers between worlds. But this was different. This was stronger, clearer, and more direct than anything I had felt before. The whisper in my mind was growing louder, more insistent, urging me to look past the surface, to dig deeper than anyone else had. It wasn't just a feeling anymore; it was a command. The land was asking me to uncover what had been buried—whether it had been overlooked or deliberately concealed. I didn't yet know.

The lives lost in that landslide weighed on me—hundreds of families, their futures swept away in a moment. I could feel the sorrow, the anger, the unresolved grief clinging to the land, as if the hills themselves had absorbed the pain of those who had perished. It wasn't just a physical scar; it was an emotional and spiritual wound, still raw and aching. The land had become a vessel for those feelings, holding onto them, waiting for someone to listen. And somehow, I knew that someone was me.

An unfamiliar sense of empathy flooded through me. I could feel the souls who had been lost, their longing for peace, for release from the torment that had bound them to this place. It was overwhelming, but not frightening—if anything, it was comforting. For the first time in a long time, I felt understood. The land, in its quiet way, was speaking to a part of me I had kept hidden for so long. A part of me that was now waking up.

The hills stood silent before me, but I knew they held the answers I had been searching for. Not just to the strange happenings in the house, but to something much larger—something buried deep beneath the soil, beneath the lies and corruption that had taken root here. The land had seen it all—the greed, the cover-ups—and it was time for the truth to come to light.

A surge of determination swept through me, solidifying into a purpose I hadn't known I was searching for. It wasn't solely for a fresh start I came to Wayanad. I had been drawn here, to these hills, to uncover the secrets buried in the earth and expose the darkness that had shrouded this place for too long. I wasn't just here for myself anymore. My purpose was to bring light to the land, to give voice to the untold stories, and to release the souls still trapped in the shadows.

As I stood there, the wind picked up, cool and insistent, carrying with it something more than just a breeze. It was faint, almost an echo, but it was there—a whisper from the past, threading through the air like a reminder that this land wasn't just broken physically. It was wounded emotionally, spiritually. The hills that once stood as symbols of life, of beauty, had become a graveyard—a resting place for the forgotten, the forsaken. But something stirred inside me, a quiet understanding that these hills didn't have to remain in darkness. They could heal. If the truth buried beneath them could finally be brought to light, there could be release, peace—not just for the land, but for the souls it held.

The whisper in my mind shifted. It was no longer soft, no longer a mere suggestion. It had become a demand, clear and undeniable—a call to action that I couldn't turn away from. The land had chosen me; I realized that now. Chosen me to be its voice, to dig up its secrets, to set right what had been wronged. I didn't know why, but I could feel the weight of that responsibility settling into me, solid and immovable.

A deep resolve welled up inside me as I finally turned away from the hills, the wind still tugging at my hair, my clothes. My mind buzzed with possibilities, plans, questions. I didn't know exactly what I was going to uncover, but I knew that the journey ahead was going to be anything but simple. There would be obstacles—fear, doubt, maybe even danger—but the purpose I felt here was stronger than all of that.

Whatever lay ahead, I couldn't look back. This was my path now. The land had called me, and I was ready to answer.

ॐ

My investigation began with a focus and fervor I hadn't felt in years. I spent hours at the local library, pouring over archives that had gathered dust for decades. I uncovered faded newspaper clippings, old photographs with edges curling from age, and forgotten books whose pages had turned brittle with time. The deeper I went, the more disturbing the picture became.

The landslide had come without warning, a monstrous force of nature that had swallowed entire villages in its path. Names like Mundakkai and Chooralmala popped up in nearly every report I found—once thriving communities, now nothing more than rubble buried beneath the earth. The stories were haunting. Torrential rains had loosened the hills, and when they gave way, they buried homes, families, lives. The survivors' accounts chilled me to the bone: parents losing sight of their children, whole families wiped out in an instant, houses crushed as though they were made of paper.

Every detail painted a more vivid picture of the disaster. The very ground I walked on wasn't just dirt and stone; it was a graveyard. And as I read, I could almost hear the voices, feel the terror of that day—the way the earth had consumed everything in its path, leaving behind only devastation.

But it wasn't just the landslide that gnawed at me. There was something darker hiding beneath the surface, something tied to the present, not just the past. As I read more about the housing society I now lived in, the pieces fell into place, and what I uncovered left me sickened. Ravi Verma—the real estate tycoon behind the development—wasn't just another visionary transforming empty land into urban marvels. No, his work masked a far more sinister reality.

The permits for the development had been rushed through, barely scrutinized. Environmental assessments had been conducted, but their findings buried, ignored, swept aside in favor of profit. Local activists who had dared to raise concerns were silenced, intimidated into retreat. The more I dug, the more I realized that Verma and his corporation had built this community on the ruins of lives, choosing to erase the pain, the memories, the sanctity of the land itself in their pursuit of wealth.

This housing society wasn't just another project—it was a monument to greed, built on the graves of the people who had perished. And as I connected the dots, I knew that the land had chosen me for a reason. It wasn't just about uncovering a mystery anymore—it was about justice. The lives lost, the souls trapped here—they hadn't found peace.

And I was the only one who could set things right.

My research consumed me. I wandered through the overgrown ruins of Mundakkai and Chooralmala, where once-thriving villages had been swallowed by the wilderness. The silence was thick, oppressive, as if the land itself was holding its breath, waiting for someone to listen. As I stood there among the crumbling remnants, I could feel the weight of the stories left untold. The surrounding air seemed to hum with the voices of those who had once called this place home—echoes of laughter, of life, now replaced by an endless mourning sigh. It was as though their presence lingered, trapped between worlds, waiting for someone to recognize their existence.

The names in the reports had become real to me. These weren't just statistics. They were families, children, people who had been full of hopes and dreams, all violently torn away in a matter of moments. I felt a suffocating connection to them, like their spirits were reaching out, seeking justice, or maybe just acknowledgment of the lives they had lived and lost. It was impossible to look away now. The more I learned, the more I felt their pain.

The further I dug, the clearer it became that the housing society had been built on more than just stolen earth—it was built on lies, on carefully constructed half-truths meant to conceal a much darker history. This land wasn't just scarred by the disaster; it was marked by human greed, exploitation, and a deliberate effort to bury the past along with the bodies. But the past doesn't stay buried forever. It surfaces to demand attention. And I had become its conduit.

My connection to the land deepened with each passing day. What had started as a strange pull had grown into something much more profound. It was as if the land itself had chosen me to be its voice, to speak for the souls that had been silenced. I wasn't just uncovering history for the sake of curiosity—I was unraveling a story that needed to be told, a truth that had been hidden for too long. With each new piece of the puzzle, I felt a stronger resolve building inside me. This wasn't just about setting the record straight. It was about justice for those who could no longer fight for themselves.

But it wasn't just the ruins, or the forgotten reports that held me in their grip. It was the energy of the land itself. The same eerie sensations I had tried so hard to ignore for years were now undeniable. The ground beneath me was alive with restless spirits, the energies of those lost to the landslide still woven into the soil. Their pain, their fear, their unresolved trauma—it was all there, beneath the surface, waiting to be acknowledged, to be set free.

I had stumbled upon something far bigger than I had expected. This was no longer just a quest to understand what had happened. It was a journey into the heart of a darkness that could fester for far too long. And I was determined to bring it to light. The spirits weren't just haunting the land; they were calling to me, asking me to be their voice, their advocate. And I couldn't turn away from them now.

IV
Visions and Revelations

The deeper I sank into the history of this land, the more my abilities—ones I had long tried to push aside—emerged. At first, it was just a faint unease, a shiver when I read about the landslide's aftermath, a tightness in my chest as I pieced together the lives lost. But soon, the sensations escalated, transforming into vivid, inescapable visions that overtook my waking moments.

It happened one evening as I sat in my study, poring over old news clippings. The room had always been my sanctuary, a place where I could focus, where I could feel grounded. But that night, something shifted. The air grew thick, like I was breathing through water, and the soft light from the lamp seemed to dim. I blinked, tried to steady myself, but the world around me dissolved.

Suddenly, I wasn't in my study anymore. I was standing in the devastation's heart left by the landslide. The ground beneath my feet felt unstable, trembling as if it might give way at any moment. Dust filled the air, thick and choking, burning my throat and stinging my eyes. All around me, the village lay in ruins—homes splintered into nothing, trees uprooted and scattered like matchsticks, the earth itself ripped apart by the force of nature.

Then I heard them—voices. They weren't just distant sounds carried on the wind; they were cries of raw, desperate terror. It was overwhelming, a flood of anguish and pleading, the voices of people who knew they were about to die. I spun around, trying to locate them, but the devastation surrounded me, and the voices came from everywhere. The cries weren't just sounds—they were soaked in emotion, vibrating with fear, pain, and the hopelessness of knowing there was no escape.

The vision blurred, and faces materialized from the dust. A young mother clutched her child, her eyes wide with horror as the ground swallowed them both. An elderly man lay trapped beneath the wreckage of his home, his hand outstretched, trembling with the last ounce of strength he could muster. Children, who should've been playing in the sunshine, instead ran screaming as the hillside gave way, their innocent joy replaced by terror. It wasn't just destruction I was witnessing—it was the last moments of their lives flashing before me in agonizing clarity.

But there was more to it than just the physical horror. I could feel it—an oppressive, malevolent force lurking beneath the surface. This wasn't just a landslide; there was something darker at play, a suffocating malevolence that had stained the land itself. The souls lost in the disaster weren't at rest. Their suffering had soaked into the earth like a wound that refused to heal, leaving them trapped in a cycle of torment, bound to this place, unable to move on.

The vision left me shaken, gasping for breath. I was back in my study, the lamp still flickering, my hands trembling. But I wasn't the same. The terror, the sorrow, the unbearable loss—it wasn't just a glimpse into the past. It was alive, pressing against me, begging for resolution. The emotions I felt were so intense, so real, that they threatened to drown me. These weren't just memories—they were still happening, still crying out for someone to hear them, to help them.

But even amidst the chaos and the darkness, I felt a strange clarity. These visions weren't meant to terrify me into paralysis. They were a call to action, a plea from the past that I couldn't ignore. The spirits of those who had died in the landslide—they weren't resting, and they had chosen me to help them. I had been given this ability for a reason, and now I had to face the truth: it was my responsibility to uncover what had been buried and to bring peace to those restless souls.

There was no turning back now. The land, the spirits, they had called me for a reason. And I was going to answer. Each day, the connection between me and the land deepened, the subtle energies that once felt like whispers now forming coherent, deliberate messages. What I had once thought were fragments of my imagination now felt like conversations—urgent, purposeful. The spirits were no longer distant; they were present, their emotions, their pain, and their hopes flowing through me like a current. The ability I had long considered a curse shifted, transforming into something powerful, something I could use. It wasn't just about speaking with the dead—it was about understanding them, helping them, and through that, healing the land they were bound to.

As I moved through the ruins, pieced together stories from the past, and sat with the silence of the hills, I felt a growing sense of clarity. The path ahead, though dark, was one I knew I had to follow. There was no turning away anymore. The tragedies of the past had become a part of my journey, and I was ready to confront whatever lay beneath the surface, no matter how difficult it might be. I was not just uncovering the land's secrets—I was giving a voice to those who had been silenced, and in doing so, I was becoming intertwined with the fate of this place.

Yet, I did not know how far this journey would take me. I wasn't just pulling back the veil on the land's history; I was stepping into a world that would challenge everything I thought I knew. The spirits weren't just asking for peace; they were pulling me into something far larger than I could have imagined. As I pressed on, I realized that this was not just about them—it was about me. This journey would strip away my understanding of life, death, and everything in between, forcing me to confront not just the spirits, but the very essence of who I was.

I could sense that the truth was close, but I also felt the weight of it looming. Whatever I uncovered would come at a cost—a test of my strength, my beliefs, and my soul. The connection I felt with the land and its spirits was not just a calling; it was a bond that would reshape me, forever altering how I saw the world. The land had chosen me for this purpose, but I knew that once I uncovered the truth, there would be no going back. And I wasn't sure what would be left of me when the journey was finally over.

What had once been a lively, hopeful community had taken a sharp turn toward something far more unsettling. The air of excitement that had filled the housing society in its early days had given way to a growing tension. Conversations that had once been filled with optimism about plans had shifted into whispered discussions about strange, inexplicable events. Neighbors who had been fast friends now exchanged uneasy glances, speaking in hushed tones about shadowy figures lurking at the edges of their vision, unexplained chills that seeped into rooms, and noises in the night that couldn't be traced to any logical source.

At first, I dismissed it. Moving into a new place, especially one with a tragic history like this, was bound to stir the imagination. People were adjusting, perhaps even carrying the weight of the land's history in ways they didn't fully understand. It seemed natural that some would feel uneasy. But as more people offered the same stories, their accounts eerily similar, I could no longer brush it off as simple nerves.

The neighborhood gatherings, which had once been full of laughter and shared dreams, took on a darker tone. What had been a chance to bond and build community had morphed into something more like a support group, a place for people to confess their growing fears about the strange occurrences that had disrupted their lives. The smiles had faded. People spoke in low, tremulous voices, casting furtive glances around the room as if expecting to see something lurking just beyond the circle of light.

One evening, as the sun sank behind the hills, painting long shadows across the neighborhood, I listened to the Murthys—a young couple who had been among the first to move in. Their faces were pale, their eyes haunted. "It started a few weeks ago," Mr. Murthy said, his voice barely more than a whisper. "We'd see these... figures, at the end of our hallway. Shadowy, like they were there but not really there. They never get close. They just stand there, watching. And when we try to approach, they vanish." He rubbed his forehead, his fingers shaking. "It's like they're waiting for something. But what could they possibly want from us?"

I felt a cold shiver run through me, but I remained quiet, listening.

Mrs. Nair, a retired schoolteacher known for her no-nonsense approach to life, spoke next. She was always so precise, so grounded—if anyone could explain away these experiences, it should have been her. But as she spoke, her usually firm voice trembled. "It always happens in the living room," she said, glancing around as if to reassure herself she was still safe. "The air turns chilly, like a freezer door has swung open, but the thermostat never changes. I've checked the windows, the doors—everything is sealed, locked tight. But the cold... it's like something's standing there, watching, just out of sight. And then, just as quickly, the warmth returns. But I'm left with this... this feeling, like I'm not alone. Like something is still there, even when I can't see it."

Her words sent a ripple of discomfort through the room. I could feel it too, that creeping sensation of being watched, the same oppressive energy that had shadowed my own days.

It was becoming harder to deny what was happening. These weren't just overactive imaginations or strange coincidences. Something was wrong. The land beneath our feet held secrets that refused to stay buried, and it was becoming clear that those secrets were bleeding through the cracks. The whispers, the shadows, the cold... they were all signs that whatever had been disturbed here would not rest until it was acknowledged.

As I sat there, listening to my neighbor's voice their fears, I realized this wasn't just a haunting—it was a reckoning.

Listening to my neighbors speak, I felt an unsettling chill of recognition. The things they described—the cold spots, the shadows lingering at the edge of vision, the overwhelming sense of being watched—it was everything I had felt too. It became painfully clear that these weren't just isolated incidents. There was a pattern, and it was growing darker by the day. Whatever was happening here, it wasn't confined to just one home or one family. It was everywhere, woven into the very walls of this housing society, seeping out from the ground beneath our feet.

Determined to understand it, I began visiting my neighbors more frequently, engaging them in conversations about their experiences. With each visit, I noted the energy in their homes, the subtle differences, and the eerie consistencies. Shadows seemed to gather in the corners. The temperature fluctuated unnervingly, and there was always that same oppressive sensation—like the land itself was pressing down on us. I meticulously documented their accounts: shadowy figures, phantom footsteps, inexplicable noises. But one thing was becoming terrifyingly clear—this wasn't just a haunted house or two. The land was alive with something, and it was not resting.

One of the most unnerving experiences came when I visited the Patel family. They had recently reported strange sounds coming from their attic—footsteps, the creak of old wood, and that ever-present feeling of eyes watching them from above. They had checked it countless times, found nothing, but the noises persisted. The tension in their home was palpable, and I could see the fear in their eyes as they asked for my help.

When I climbed the narrow staircase leading to the attic, the air became heavy, each step weighed down by a suffocating presence. As I reached the top, the temperature plummeted dramatically, my breath hanging in the air in cold, misty clouds. The small, dirty windows barely let in any light, casting long, sinister shadows. I could feel it then—the presence. Something was here, something aware of me, something that didn't want me there. I tried to push forward, but my body felt sluggish, as though the very air had turned against me. Shadows moved in the corners of my vision, quick, fleeting, but unmistakable.

This was no ordinary haunting. Whatever was in that attic—it was powerful, and it wanted to be known.

After that experience, the patterns I'd been seeing became impossible to ignore. These weren't just random hauntings or ghost stories. They were manifestations of a deep, unresolved tragedy, a sorrow that had soaked into the land itself. The spirits of those who had died in the landslide weren't at peace. Their lives, violently cut short, had left echoes—resonating through time, their pain and loss tethering them to this place. And now, the living were feeling the weight of that unresolved grief.

Seeking more answers, I turned to Mrs. Varma, a local historian who had spent years documenting the area's past. When I told her about the disturbances, she listened carefully; her weathered face was grim. She handed me old maps, faded records, and photographs yellowed with age—documents from a time before the disaster had wiped everything away. These weren't just relics; they were the remnants of a community that had once been vibrant and full of life, obliterated in an instant, leaving behind not just physical ruins, but a profound and lingering sorrow.

As she showed me an old photograph of the village now buried beneath the land, Mrs. Varma's voice was quiet, almost reverent. "The land remembers," she said, her fingers tracing the lines of the map. "The soil here is steeped in sorrow, as though the earth itself weeps for those who cannot move on."

Her words hung in the air, heavy with truth. The land wasn't just a graveyard of bodies—it was a graveyard of emotions, of lives and futures that had been stolen. The earth itself had absorbed their pain, and now that pain was spilling out, demanding to be acknowledged. It wasn't just the houses or the society that was haunted—it was the land itself, crying out for justice, for peace. And somehow, I had become part of that cry.

I left Mrs. Varma's home with a deeper understanding, but also with a gnawing dread. This wasn't something that could be easily fixed or cleansed. The spirits weren't just restless; they were calling for something—resolution, acknowledgment, perhaps even vengeance. And until the truth of what had happened here was fully uncovered, neither the living nor the dead would find peace.

As I absorbed the weight of these revelations, it became clearer than ever that the spirits haunting this place weren't here out of malice or formless rage. They were tethered, bound to the land in the wake of the violent rupture that tore their lives apart. The land, once peaceful and vibrant, had been transformed by trauma, its serenity shattered. And now, the housing society—shiny and modern on the surface—sat like a fragile bandage over a wound that had never healed, its glossy façade covering the cracks and bleeding pain that still pulsed beneath.

Recognizing the disturbances wasn't enough anymore. I couldn't just bear witness to the eerie manifestations and haunted whispers. There was a deeper calling—a duty to engage with these spirits and help them find peace, to guide them toward the closure they had been denied for so long. Their pain had become part of the land itself, a cry that echoed through every shadow, every cold gust of wind. And I had to be the one to listen.

With a clear sense of purpose, I began planning a plan. I would have to connect with the spirits in a way that acknowledged their existence, their pain. To do this, I needed more than just my own experiences—I needed the stories of those who had lived through the landslide, those whose lives had been irrevocably changed. Their voices, I hoped, would offer insight into the spiritual weight that still hung over this place.

I started a series of interviews with landslide survivors, hoping to uncover the emotional and spiritual scars left behind by the disaster. Each story was heartbreaking, filled with unbearable loss and the trauma that leaves people tethered to the past in ways they can't explain.

Pranjeesh, a survivor from Mundakkai, spoke to me in a voice heavy with sorrow, as if the weight of his memories had hollowed him out. "The sound of the landslide... that roar... it never leaves me," he said, his eyes distant, filled with a pain that time had not eased. "I lost my aunt and her entire family. I hear them every night, Aadhira. Screaming. Crying for help. It's like... it's like they're still out there, waiting for someone to save them."

His words sent a shiver through me, confirming what I had suspected—that the spirits were trapped in those final, desperate moments, replaying the terror of their deaths over and over.

Prasanna, another survivor, shared a story that shook me to my core. She had been frantically searching for her sister and her children the night of the landslide, but they had been swallowed by the rushing earth, lost in the darkness. "I only saved my father. I carried him through the forest. But my sister, her children... I couldn't find them," she said, her voice thick with grief as she fought to keep from breaking down. "In my dreams, I hear them. They call out to me, begging me to find them, but I can't. I can't."

As I listened to Prasanna, her words reverberated with the same desperate cry that haunted me from the spirits I felt in the land. The restless souls weren't just wandering—they were lost, caught in the agony of their last moments, waiting for someone to acknowledge them, to remember their names, their faces, their lives.

Each story I gathered brought me closer to the truth. These spirits weren't angry or vengeful—they were desperate for recognition. They were mothers, fathers, children who had spent their last moments in terror, in confusion, with their futures torn from them in an instant. And now, they were tied to the earth, their unresolved pain seeping into the soil itself, crying out for someone to hear them.

As I pieced together these fragmented stories, the weight of my responsibility grew. These spirits weren't just memories—they were still here, trapped in the land's fabric, unable to move on because their lives had ended so violently, so unjustly. And the more I learned, the more I understood: I was here not just to uncover the truth, but to help them find peace. I was their bridge between the past and the present, the living and the dead. It was up to me to acknowledge their pain, to give them a voice, and to guide them toward the closure they had been denied for so long.

The land wasn't just haunted—it was crying for justice. And I could feel its plea pressing down on me, urging me forward. I wasn't sure how I would help them find peace, but I knew I couldn't turn away from the responsibility that had been placed upon me.

As twilight deepened and cast its purple hue across the sky, I gathered the residents for a meeting—something that had been building inside me for weeks. The air was heavy with anticipation, and I could feel the weight of what I was about to say pressing down on me. But I knew it had to be done. The time confronted the truth of what was happening beneath our feet, to acknowledge the past that had been crying out for so long, demanding to be heard.

When I spoke, I did so carefully, choosing my words with conviction. "The disturbances we're experiencing aren't just accidents, and they aren't figments of our imagination," I began, my voice steady even though I could feel the tension in the room. "The very ground our homes are built on is steeped in sorrow and loss. We need to acknowledge the pain that's rooted here. We need to give voice to those who've been silenced for so long."

The room fell silent, the air thick with unease and understanding. I could see it in their faces—the weight of recognition. The same unsettling experiences they had been trying to rationalize now had a name, a cause. The spirits of the past were not just restless, they were seeking acknowledgment. They needed to be remembered, to be honored.

I took a breath and proposed what I had been planning. "Let's hold a ceremony," I urged. "A collective memorial for the lives lost in the landslide. We owe it to them—and to ourselves—to honor their memory. We need to acknowledge the tragedy that happened here and help bring peace to the spirits tied to this land. Only then can we move forward."

For a long moment, no one spoke. The room was filled with a quiet tension as the residents absorbed my words. Some nodded, their expressions filled with a quiet resolve, understanding that this was something they needed to face. But others exchanged uneasy glances, reluctant to confront what they had spent so long ignoring. The thought of facing the spirits walking among them, of addressing the pain rooted in this land, was daunting.

But even in the uncertainty, I could feel a shift. There was a sense of purpose slowly building in the room, a cautious hope that maybe, just maybe, this ceremony could offer the closure they all needed. By facing the past, we could heal the present.

As the meeting ended, and the residents slowly dispersed into the evening, I stood for a moment longer in the fading light. The weight of what was to come settled over me, but it was a weight I had learned to bear. I could sense it—the land, the spirits. They were waiting for this. Waiting for someone to acknowledge them, to give them the release they deserved. And I knew that the ceremony would be more than just a memorial. It was a bridge, a way to invite the living and the dead into a shared space of understanding and healing.

The path ahead would be difficult. The spirits needed more than just words; they needed a true, heartfelt release from their suffering. But I understood that this wasn't just about them. It was about healing the land, healing the people who had built their lives upon it, and finally putting to rest the sorrow that had lingered here for so long.

The land had chosen me. That much was clear now. And I had chosen it too. As the veil between the living and the dead grew ever thinner, I knew I was the only one who could bridge that gap. And for the first time, I felt ready to face the challenge. We would confront the past together—spirit and living, land and memory—and perhaps, through that confrontation, we would all find peace.

V

A Call for Help

My nights have become a blur of unsettling dreams and haunting figures. What used to be a normal existence is unraveling, as if the boundary between reality and the supernatural no longer matters. Every night, the line grows thinner, and now, I can't tell where one ends and the other begins. It's in these twilight hours that she comes—a girl, only twelve, glowing faintly as if made of light. But it's her eyes that seize me—deep, sorrowful, and filled with an urgency I can't shake.

At first, she was just a flicker in the corner of my eye. I'd see her on the edge of mirrors, disappearing before I could fully register her. Sometimes, I'd hear my name—soft, like a breath on the wind—sending a chill up my spine. Every time she came, I felt her eyes on me. More than that, I felt pulled, like she needed me to follow, to understand something I wasn't yet ready to see.

One evening, after another night of barely sleeping, I sat by the window, staring out into the fog-drenched streets. The silence in the house was suffocating, the distant hum of traffic the only reminder that I wasn't completely alone.

And then there she was. Not a glimpse this time, but a full apparition, standing outside my window. Her eyes locked on mine, and for a moment, the world seemed to stop. The sorrow in her gaze was overwhelming, and the urgency... I could feel it in my bones.

Without thinking, I grabbed my coat and stepped into the night. The air was cool, filled with the scent of wet earth, and the streetlights flickered, casting eerie shadows that twisted along the pavement. Every step felt like I was walking through a dream I had lived before—familiar yet distant. I didn't know where I was going, but I couldn't stop.

She led me deeper into the forgotten corners of the housing society, where everything felt abandoned and left to rot. The streets gave way to overgrown patches of land, tangled with vines and forgotten by time. The air felt heavy, and the surrounding silence thickened until it was almost unbearable. And then, I saw it—the old wall, hidden by the overgrowth, the last remnant of something ancient, something far older than this place.

I stood there, breath shallow, my heart pounding as the girl hovered near the wall. Her eyes were still on me, sorrowful, relentless. She raised her hand and pointed at the ground. My chest tightened—I knew what she wanted me to see.

I knelt, fingers brushing against the cold, damp earth. The surrounding air shifted, like the past itself was crying out, pressing down on me. There was something here—something buried not just in the ground, but in the history of this place, in the pain and lives that had been lost.

The girl lingered for a moment longer before fading into the mist, leaving me alone with whatever truth I was about to uncover. I didn't know what I would find beneath the soil, but I knew one thing for sure: it held the key to everything—the spirits, the land, and the tragedy that bound them all.

My hands trembled as I pushed aside the thicket of brambles that had grown wild around the crumbling stones. My heart pounded with a mix of dread and expectation as my fingers scraped against the weathered surface of the wall, finally unearthing a small, forgotten plaque.

The inscription, though worn and faded, was still legible: "In memory of those who were lost and never found."

An icy wave of realization crashed over me. This forgotten, overgrown plot wasn't just neglected land—it was an unmarked burial site. The last resting place of those who had been claimed by the landslide, whose bodies were never recovered. In the aftermath of that disaster, they had been hurriedly buried and just as quickly forgotten. But their spirits, disturbed and left unrested, had been crying out all this time, reaching for acknowledgment, for peace. The housing society had been built over their grave, unknowingly desecrating the very ground where they lay, and it was their torment that had bled into the present, haunting everyone who lived here.

As I stood there, the girl's figure reappeared, hovering just a few feet away. Her face was translucent, but the emotion on it was unmistakable—a mix of sorrow and relief. She didn't speak, but her presence was enough to convey her message. She was one of them, one of the lost souls, and she had come to me not out of malice, but out of a desperate need for someone to help. To be seen. To be remembered.

I looked at her, my chest tight with emotion, and in that moment, I understood the depth of their suffering. These souls had been bound to this land by tragedy, their pain and despair anchoring them here, unable to move on. The violent rupture of their lives had left a wound on the earth that had never healed, and in the rush to modernize and rebuild, they had been forsaken.

A sense of purpose surged within me, clear and resolute. I knew what had to be done. The land, the spirits, the forgotten—they needed more than just acknowledgment. They needed peace. It wasn't just about exorcising a haunting or quieting restless souls. It was about honoring the memory of those who had been lost, giving them the closure they had been denied for so long.

Beside the plaque, I knelt, feeling the cold, damp earth as my fingers brushed against it. "I see you", my voice trembling. "I will help you find peace." The girl's figure flickered, her expression softening, and for the first time since I had encountered her, I felt a shift—like the first sign of healing.

To bring peace to the haunted lands of Wayanad, I would need to confront the past head-on. The community had to come together, not just to remember, but to honor the lives that had been lost. We would need to hold the ceremony, but it had to be more than symbolic. It had to be real. The pain of the past could no longer be ignored or forgotten. I had to ensure that these spirits would finally be released from their torment, their memories honored, and their connection to this land healed.

The path ahead would not be easy, but I felt ready. The land had chosen me, and now I was ready to answer the call. For the spirits, for the land, and for the people who lived here, I would be the one to bridge the gap between the past and the present. The healing could begin.

The weight of what I had uncovered pressed down on me, heavier with each passing second. The unmarked burial site wasn't just a secret—it was a truth that could no longer be hidden. It wasn't only mine to carry; it belonged to everyone who lived here, whose homes had been built over this land steeped in sorrow and loss. The spirits weren't just haunting me—they were crying out to all of us.

I had to tell them.

I gathered the residents in the community hall, the mood was as heavy as I felt. The room was small, plain, with freshly painted white walls that did nothing to lift the tension thickening the air. The fluorescent lights buzzed overhead, sharp and unkind, casting harsh shadows on the faces that slowly filled the rows of metal chairs. I could see it in their eyes—concern, curiosity, and a growing, gnawing fear. They knew something was wrong, had felt it for some time, but no one had been willing to name it. Now, it was up to me.

As I stood in front of them, I took a deep breath. My voice sounded steady, but inside, I felt the gravity of the moment pulling at me. "I've discovered something," I began, my eyes scanning the room, catching on familiar faces. "Something that affects us all." I paused, letting the weight of my words settle over them. "There's an unmarked burial site near the edge of our society. It's where many of the landslide victims were buried hastily, as a temporary measure. But their remains were never retrieved. They were left there. And now... their spirits haven't found peace. What we've been feeling in our homes—the cold, the shadows—it's them. It's those lost souls trying to be heard."

A hush fell over the room, heavy and oppressive. Disbelief flickered in their eyes, but something else too—recognition. They had sensed this, deep down, even if they hadn't wanted to admit it. Now, it was staring them in the face.

Prasanna was the first to speak. She stood slowly, her face pale, grief carved into every line. I knew her story—everyone here did. She had lost her sister and her two young children in the landslide. That kind of pain never fades, never heals completely. Her voice trembled, the emotion in it raw and palpable. "I still hear their screams in my dreams," she said, her voice breaking under the weight of her words. Tears welled up in her eyes, and her hands shook as she spoke. "I was so close when it happened. I could hear them, feel the ground collapsing around us. But I couldn't reach them. I couldn't save them."

Her voice, thick with anguish, cut through the silence like a blade, sharp and excruciating. The room seemed to hold its breath. Every person there felt the pain in her words, a reminder of the grief that had touched so many lives in this place. It wasn't just Prasanna's loss—it was the land's, and it had been echoing through the ground beneath us for years.

I watched as the truth settled over them. This wasn't just a story about the past. It was happening now. The spirits were here, crying out for recognition, for peace. And we, the living, had been ignoring them for too long.

I approached Prasanna slowly, placing a gentle hand on her shoulder. Her sobs quieted as I leaned closer. "Prasanna," I said softly, "their spirits linger because their lives weren't properly honored. We can change that. We can give them the peace they were denied." Her breathing steadied, and though her eyes were still wet with tears, I could see a flicker of understanding in her expression, a tentative resolve settling within her.

As Prasanna sank back into her seat, another voice broke the silence. Raghav—a man known for his rationality, a skeptic who rarely entertained talk of the supernatural—looked visibly shaken. His usual stern composure faltered, and his eyes, filled with smoldering unease, betrayed his internal struggle.

"I've seen them too," he admitted, his deep voice strained with uncharacteristic hesitation. "Strange shadows, flickering in my backyard at night. At first, I thought it was just my mind playing tricks. But then... there's this cold spot in my home, right where my daughter used to play. It's as if... someone else is there. Someone reaching out."

His confession sent a chill through the room. I felt it too—a shiver that ran through me as the weight of what he was saying settled in. It wasn't just the odd occurrences anymore; these were actual experiences, and they were undeniable.

"These spirits are trying to communicate with us, Raghav," I said, my voice firm but empathetic. "They're not here by choice. They're bound to this place because their final resting place was neglected, violated. If we want to help them, we have to acknowledge them, and release them from this suffering."

The room, which had been heavy with disbelief and uncertainty, now buzzed with a new energy—a collective understanding that something much larger, much darker, had been beneath their feet all along. The unease they had been feeling wasn't something to be dismissed anymore. It was real, and it demanded action.

Prasanna, her tears now wiped away, lifted her head and looked around the room. Her voice, though still thick with emotion, was filled with newfound strength. "We have all suffered," she said, her gaze moving from face to face.

"Maybe this is our chance—a chance to make peace with the past, to bring some solace to the spirits who were wronged, and to ourselves."

A murmur of agreement spread through the group. I could feel it, a shift—a sense of collective responsibility taking root. Each one of them knew, deep down, that they were connected to this land and the history buried beneath it. Now it was time to confront that truth and do something about it.

This was no longer just about hauntings or disturbances. It was about making things right. And we were ready to face it, together.

Raghav nodded, his expression resolute. "If this is what's needed to bring peace—not just for the spirits, but for us, too—then we do it. We owe them that."

The room, once thick with fear and uncertainty, now buzzed with a distinct energy. A sense of purpose, of shared responsibility, had settled over the residents. Together, we discussed the plan—a memorial ceremony at the unmarked burial site. This would not be just an act of remembrance, but a ritual of healing. Healing for the spirits still bound to this land, and for all of us, too.

We lit candles for those who had perished, each flame a guide to help the lost souls find their way home. Prayers would be offered, not just from one tradition, but from many—each voice weaving together a chorus of hope, calling out for peace. Stories would be shared, memories brought to life again, so that those lost would no longer be forgotten, their names and lives carried forward by those who remained.

As the meeting came to a close, the feeling in the room had shifted entirely. Where there had once been dread and hesitation, now there was unity and resolve. The fear had not disappeared, but it had transformed into something more—something that felt like hope.

I could feel it, too. As I looked around at the faces of my neighbors, I realized that this was more than a ceremony for the dead. It was for us, too. We had all been affected by the tragedies buried beneath our homes, even if we hadn't understood it until now. By acknowledging the spirits, by honoring their lives, we would also heal ourselves.

The path ahead was clear, and though it would be difficult, I knew we were ready. Together, we would face the past, and in doing so, we might finally find peace—for them, and for us.

☙

The day of the memorial came quietly, bringing with it a sense of somber tranquility, laced with the faintest whisper of hope. We gathered at the old, unmarked burial site, each of us carrying a small candle or a simple floral tribute—symbols of our memories, our grief, and the peace we longed to offer. The air felt fresh, heavy with meaning, and as we walked together in silence, our steps seemed to echo with the shared weight of the mission ahead.

I led the group to the site, and as twilight settled, casting an otherworldly gloom over the land, the tiny flames of our candles flickered gently against the darkness. There was something comforting in that light, something that felt like a promise—that our act of remembrance was a protective force against the shadows of the past, against the pain that had lingered here for so long.

One by one, we lit our candles, forming a glowing circle around the uncovered plaque, each flame a quiet dedication to those who had been lost. The ceremony unfolded in soft whispers and quiet resolve. Some shared stories—memories of loved ones, of lives cut short by the landslide's unforgiving force. These weren't just recollections; they were bridges, invisible threads that reached across time, pulling the past into the present, connecting the living with the dead.

As I listened, I felt something shift in the air. It wasn't just grief anymore—it was something else. Reconciliation. As each story was spoken, as each name was remembered, it felt as though we were mending a tear in the fabric of this place. Each word, each memory shared, became a stitch, slowly closing the breach that had formed between worlds, healing the wound left by that long-ago tragedy.

Standing there, I felt a unity that words can't quite describe. It was in the quiet murmurs of the gathered community, in the way the flames danced softly around the site, in the way the darkness seemed to pull back just a little. There was an energy in the air, something palpable and powerful. It was grief, yes, but it was also hope. It was the raw power of collective intention—the power that could soothe restless spirits, that could turn sorrow into peace.

And in that moment, as I looked at the faces of my neighbors, as I felt the shared purpose that bound us together, I knew. We weren't just offering remembrance; we were offering healing. To the spirits, to the land, and to ourselves.

We were telling those lost souls, "You are seen. You are remembered. You are honored."

As the last story faded into the quiet night, and the last candle flickered to life, the surrounding air shifted. The oppressive heaviness that had weighed us down for months seemed to lift, dissipating like a mist burned away by the sun. In its place was a softer, gentler presence, as if the spirits had finally felt our offering, had heard the words spoken in their honor. It wasn't dramatic, but it was undeniable—a sense of calm, of peace, settling over the land. The spirits, at least for now, had found what they had been yearning for—a path to rest.

There was a quiet, shared acknowledgment in the air—a subdued joy, not the kind that sparkles with excitement, but the kind that comes from a deep sense of relief. We had done something good. The circle of candles, glowing softly against the encroaching night, the whispered stories and shared grief—they lingered as symbols of this new beginning. We had given the lost souls a chance to rest, and in doing so, had lightened our own burden.

As the residents left the site, there was a shift among them. I could see it in the way they moved, the way they glanced at one another—a renewed sense of purpose. We weren't just neighbors anymore, bound by proximity and shared walls. We had become something more, connected by this shared experience, by the act of healing not just ourselves, but the land and the restless souls that had been trapped here for so long.

I felt it too. This ceremony had been a turning point, a necessary first step in what would undoubtedly be a longer journey. There was still work to be done, still more spirits to honor, more stories to unearth. The energy of the land hadn't completely settled, and I knew there would be more confrontations ahead—more moments where we would need to face the shadows of the past head-on. But now, we wouldn't be doing it alone. The community stood behind me, unified by a common goal: to bring peace to Wayanad, to the living and the dead alike.

As I stood there, watching the candles flicker one last time before they were swallowed by the night, I felt a quiet hope stirring in me. This was the beginning of a new chapter—a chapter of healing, of remembrance, of honoring the restless spirits while reclaiming our homes from the grip of the past. We weren't done yet, but we were on our way. And maybe, just maybe, this was how peace would finally come—to the land, to the spirits, and to us.

🙰

The memorial, meant to be a solemn offering of peace, unfolded with a delicate mix of reverence and hope. For a moment, as I read aloud the names of the departed, there was unity. A feeling that maybe, just maybe, our collective mourning could bring solace to the restless spirits that lingered here. The air held a stillness, a deceptive calm that lulled us all into believing we were on the verge of something meaningful, something healing.

But then, I felt it. A shift. Subtle, almost imperceptible, like the ground beneath our feet was preparing to give way. The air grew dense, thickening with an unseen weight, and it felt as though the earth itself was holding its breath. Shadows, just beyond the reach of our candles, moved—swaying, creeping closer, as though they had a will of their own. The hairs on the back of my neck stood on end as I closed my eyes, reaching out with my abilities, letting my senses drift into the ether. I could feel them—the spirits—gathering, their presence thickening the very air around us.

The temperature plummeted, a coldness unlike any natural chill, and I shivered despite myself. A gentle breeze rustled through the trees, but it carried something more—whispers. Faint, fragmented, the silenced voices of those who had been lost in the tragedy. Their sorrow and desperation clung to the air, and I knew we were not alone.

Prasanna stepped forward, tears brimming in her eyes, her face etched with the grief that had become a permanent part of her. She knelt by the grave, placing a single white rose on the soil, her voice fragile as she whispered, "This is for you, my dear ones. I will never forget you." The words broke like glass, sharp and delicate, and the pain in them was palpable. One by one, the others followed, laying down their offerings—flowers, mementos, pieces of their sorrow—until the unmarked grave was blanketed with tokens of remembrance.

And then it happened. The spirits, unseen but unmistakable, enveloped us like a fog—weightless yet inescapable. I could feel their yearning, their desperate need to be acknowledged, to be released from the torment that had bound them to this place. Their presence pressed in from all sides, heavy and mournful. I whispered a silent prayer, asking the universe to guide them to peace, to allow them the rest they had been denied for so long.

But as the last flicker of candlelight died, something shifted again. The air, which had momentarily felt lighter, now grew colder—darker. An unsettling chill settled over the housing society, deeper and more insidious than before. Whatever peace we had hoped to offer seemed to slip away, replaced by a creeping sense of dread. It was as if, instead of releasing the spirits, we had awakened something else. Something darker.

The residents, once filled with hope for closure, now exchanged uneasy glances. I could see it in their faces—the terror slowly taking root, the realization that what we had set in motion was far from over. The weight of their hope twisted into something more sinister, a silent fear that perhaps we hadn't brought peace, but stirred the restless spirits even further.

The night grew darker, colder, and the sense of unease clung to us like a shadow. We had dared to confront the past, to bring the dead into the light. But now, the night seemed to stretch on endlessly, and with it, a deeper, more dangerous force lingered, waiting in the dark.

It began quietly at first, almost as if the land itself was testing our resolve, probing the boundaries of our fragile peace. Minor disturbances—the kinds of things we might have dismissed as nothing—unsettled the routine of our lives. Items went missing, only to reappear in places no one remembered putting them. Lights flickered and dimmed without cause, their steady glow replaced by a nervous, erratic pulse. Shadows slithered along the walls, moving in ways that defied logic, as though they had developed a life of their own. The safety of our homes, once sanctuaries of warmth and comfort, had shifted, taking on an air of hostility. It felt as if the very walls were breathing, alive with something unseen but palpable.

For me, things escalated faster than I could have imagined. I woke one night to the sound of whispers—low, indistinguishable voices that seemed to echo through my apartment. They weren't words I could understand, but the desperation in them was unmistakable. The temperature dropped so suddenly that I could see my breath, and I was frozen in place, not just from the cold, but from the creeping fear that something—someone—was watching me. Out of the corner of my eye, I caught glimpses of shadowy figures, hovering just at the edge of my vision, vanishing the second I turned to face them. They were always just out of reach, always waiting.

Then came the night that sent my heart racing. I had wandered out into the deserted streets of the society, trying to shake off the growing unease that clung to me like a second skin. The air was unnaturally still, not a breath of wind to stir the trees or rustle the leaves. That's when it happened—an icy touch brushed against my arm. Cold, deliberate. I spun around, my heart hammering, but there was nothing—nothing but the dark. The streetlights cast weak, flickering halos, barely enough to hold the night at bay. And in the shadows, I saw them again—those shifting, twitching shapes, writhing as if trying to reach for me, to pull me into whatever world they inhabited. The spirits, once distant and mournful, had grown more aggressive. I could feel it—they were no longer confined to their realm. They were crossing over, pressing into mine.

I wasn't the only one. The other residents felt it too, like a ripple of fear spreading through the community, infecting each of us. Prasanna, who had once found some comfort in the memorial, now woke screaming from nightmares. But they were no longer just memories of the screams from the landslide. Her dreams had twisted into something darker, more malevolent. She described hidden places—forgotten corners of the society that seemed to call to her in a language she couldn't understand, one that was soaked in agony and despair.

Raghav, ever the skeptic, had kept the worst of the manifestations at bay. His home had remained relatively untouched—until now. His daughter's old room had changed. It had become cold, lifeless, like something had drained the warmth from it. There was a void there, a suffocating emptiness that pressed in on him whenever he crossed the threshold. The shadows in that room no longer merely moved—they took shape. They twisted and merged, forming dark, formless figures that loomed in the corners, watching him with an unsettling, almost sentient purpose.

The spirits had grown stronger. Their presence was no longer passive; it was invasive, relentless. Whatever we had stirred with the memorial had not found peace—it had awoken something far more dangerous. And now we were living in the aftermath. The past wasn't just haunting us—it was consuming us.

Days and nights blurred into one, a twisted dance of fear and uncertainty as the shadows were joined by a new terror. It started innocently enough—a phrase scrawled in one home, almost easy to dismiss as a prank. But soon, the words multiplied, seeping into the walls of house after house. "Help us. The truth is hidden. There's more to find" it read, the message trembling in childlike script, glowing faintly as if it pulsed from within the walls themselves.

At first, some of us tried to explain it away—maybe it was someone playing a sick joke. But the glowing letters weren't just a haunting sight. They seemed to burrow into our minds, resonating with the deepest fears that had festered within us. We were no longer a community seeking closure; we had become a place teetering on the edge of unraveling. Fear clung to the air like humidity before a storm, thick and suffocating. And I knew—I was at the center of it all.

Determined to uncover the truth, I began visiting the homes marked by the message. Each visit felt heavier than the last, the air growing more oppressive with each threshold I crossed. It was as if time had warped within these spaces, twisting into something otherworldly. In one house, a young mother sat trembling, clutching her child to her chest. Her eyes were wide, frantic. "It appeared overnight," she said, her voice brittle. "I thought it was just a dream. But it's there every morning... and the whispers, they never stop. It's like they're trying to tell me something—something awful."

I moved to the next house, where an elderly couple sat in eerie silence, their eyes fixed on the shadows flickering across their walls. The husband finally spoke, his voice distant, hollow. "They're watching us," he muttered. "I feel their eyes… even when mine are closed."

The message was simple—the spirits weren't just lingering anymore. They were demanding something, pushing harder, pressing for release through the only means they had left: fear.

The tension in the society reached a fever pitch. Panic spread like wildfire. What had started as whispered murmurs had become a torrent of terror. The disturbances, once sporadic and confined to individual homes, now throbbed through every corner of the community. Shadows grew longer, darker, spiraling down hallways in unnatural shapes. Doors slammed shut with the weight of finality, and pockets of cold—brutal, bone-deep cold—seemed to follow us wherever we went.

I saw it in my neighbors' eyes. They had documented every eerie sound, every object that moved on its own, trying to make sense of the madness. But the deeper we dove into the mystery, the more illogical it became. This wasn't just a haunting—it was a siege. The spirits weren't simply passing through—they were trying to break free, and the walls between their world and ours were growing thinner by the day.

The message, "There's more to find," echoed through my mind. The spirits weren't just crying out for help—they were pointing to something hidden, something darker than we had realized. And whatever it was, it wouldn't let us rest until it was unearthed.

As I stood there, watching the flickering lights and creeping shadows, I understood we had to go deeper. The memorial hadn't been enough. The spirits wanted the truth—the whole truth. Something had been buried alongside their bodies, and until it was revealed, the terror would only grow.

We weren't just haunted. We were being hunted—by the very past we had hoped to put to rest.

That night, as I sat in my living room, trying to push the dread aside, I felt it again—an icy draft that pierced my skin like needles. The lights flickered violently, casting grotesque shadows that writhed on the walls, moving as if alive, as if they had a will of their own. Then I heard it. "Aadhira…" A voice, soft yet filled with sorrow, melodic in its despair, slipped through the trembling air, settling deep in my bones.

I shot to my feet, my heart hammering in my chest. "Who are you?" I called into the suffocating silence, my voice trembling. But no response came. Instead, the world around me seemed to still, my apartment suspended between the realm of the living and the dead. The air felt heavy, oppressive. And then the whispers returned—close, too close, brushing against my skin like a breath from another world.

The message on the walls, the glowing script that had invaded our homes, was no longer just a desperate cry for help. It was a demand, a command. I could feel it, deep within me—the spirits weren't asking anymore. They were pushing me to uncover something buried, something older and darker than any of us had realized. This was no longer about the landslide or the memorials. There was a deeper, more insidious truth hidden beneath the surface, and the spirits were growing impatient. The urgency in their voices pulsed through me, igniting a fire of determination that burned brighter than the fear gripping my heart.

I couldn't sit still any longer. This wasn't a haunting that would fade with time. The spirits were leading me toward something—some truth that had been buried with them, a danger that could rip apart everything we had tried to build. Whatever hid in the shadows, it threatened more than just our present. It was unraveling the past, dragging us all toward something terrifyingly inevitable.

I understood now. It was up to me. The burden of their voices, their cries for release, had fallen on my shoulders. The journey to uncover the buried truths had only just begun, and each step would lead me closer to a revelation I wasn't sure any of us were ready for. But I had no choice. The spirits wouldn't rest, and neither could I. This was my path now—one that could save us all or doom us forever.

With a deep breath, I steeled myself, knowing that from this moment on, every action, every decision I made, would carry the weight of both the living and the dead.

VI
Unearthing the Truth

The moon hung low over Wayanad, casting an eerie glow over the land, like a watchful eye that saw everything yet offered no comfort. I made my way back to the burial site, the weight of midnight pressing against me, the oppressive silence thickening with every step. The air felt charged, heavy with the stillness that comes before something terrible unfolds. My footsteps barely made a sound on the soft soil, but each one felt like a drumbeat in my chest, the flashlight in my hand sending shadows skittering and writhing like wounded animals, twisting across the earth as though tethered by some invisible force.

The land whispered its secrets—secrets that had been buried deep but now stirred beneath the surface, ready to break free. The memorial that was supposed to have brought closure had only cracked open something darker, something restless. I could feel it all around me. The spirits, the dead, their unseen eyes pressed down on me, their presence heavy in the air. They were no longer content to be forgotten.

I pressed forward, unwilling to turn back. The cemetery lay in disarray, the markers crooked, disheveled, almost as though the earth itself had tried to spit them out. Each grave was a reminder of the tragedy that had struck without warning. Lives cut short and buried in haste. Some graves were only marked by broken shards of pottery or hastily placed stones. I navigated the uneven ground, my flashlight flickering across patches of earth that felt as if they might open beneath my feet, pulling me into the void.

"Help us. The truth is hidden. There's more to find."

The message had become a warning, its meaning more sinister with every passing day. Those words, scrawled across the walls of nearly every home, haunted me. They weren't just a cry for help anymore. They carried with them a threat, a command, urging me deeper into the darkness that had taken root in Wayanad. The rhythm of the village had changed; fear now pulsed in the heart of every resident. Something had been unleashed, something so powerful and old that it had distorted reality itself.

For days, I had buried myself in the remnants of the past, my hands dusted with the brittle remains of old ledgers and yellowed documents that crumbled at the edges. Iron-clasped records from forgotten offices, government files stained with age and neglect, and newspaper archives left untouched for decades—all held fragments of a story that no one had wanted to remember. Piece by piece, I had unraveled a truth that had long been hidden beneath layers of deception, a truth that had unknowingly bound the spirits of the dead to the very ground where they had met their untimely end.

What I found shook me to my core.

These lands weren't just the resting place for those lost in a disaster; they were the site of a grand cover-up, a sweeping erasure of tragedy orchestrated to protect profits and reputations. Real estate developers, eager to move forward with their plans, had hurriedly buried the dead—without proper rites, without acknowledgment. They hadn't just buried bodies; they had buried the full scope of the disaster itself. Some had been laid to rest in unmarked graves, while others had simply vanished beneath the landslide, swallowed whole by the earth, with no one left to remember them.

The deeper I dug, the more the scope of the injustice revealed itself to me. I traced the paper trail across time—sifting through the layers of bureaucratic neglect, uncovering the forgotten memories of those too frightened to speak, and finding records that had been hidden for years. There were names without faces, names that had never been claimed. Government reports listed bodies that had never been identified, reduced to numbers on a page—mere statistics in a ledger that had been quietly forgotten.

With every new discovery, I felt the land tightening its grip, as though it were trying to keep its secrets buried beneath the soil. The weight of the past pressed down on me, and I realized that what we had experienced in the housing society was just the surface. The spirits weren't just restless because of the landslide. They were bound here by the injustice of it all—because their lives had been erased, their stories buried along with their bodies, their deaths reduced to something inconvenient.

It was as if the land itself had become complicit, clutching these secrets to itself, refusing to release them until someone—I—forced them into the light. The whispers

I had heard, the words scrawled on the walls, all of it had been leading to this. The spirits weren't just asking for peace. They were demanding justice. They wanted the truth to be told, their lives remembered—not as mere casualties of a disaster, but as people who had been wronged in death as much as in life.

And now, I had to decide what to do with the truth I had uncovered.

That evening, as I sat hunched over a weathered newspaper, I stumbled upon an article that detailed the aftermath of the landslides—the frantic rescue efforts, the desperate cries for help swallowed by the debris, and the unbearable search for the missing. It was a single quote from survivor Padmavathi that gripped me, sinking its teeth into my heart: "She left me alone. Who will take care of me now? I am all alone." Her words were a haunting echo of the disaster's human toll, a cry that seemed to reverberate through the decades, pressing against my mind.

The weight of those words followed me as I visited the relief camps where the displaced still lived, their grief lingering like the scent of damp earth that filled the air. These camps were a repository of untold stories, places where the human spirit was battered but still clinging to the faintest threads of survival.

One woman, Meera, a young mother clutching her child tightly to her chest, recounted her terror. She spoke through tears of the day the earth gave way; the landslide sweeping everything before it. She had run, she said, fled with her child in her arms. But her voice cracked as she remembered the helplessness, the guilt of not being able to save her neighbor, who had been lost in the mud and rubble. Her grief was raw, palpable, her tears falling like a river that had no end. "Why me?" she asked, her voice trembling. "Why did

I survive when so many didn't?"

An elderly couple told me their story next, voices heavy with guilt. They had waited on a hilltop for their neighbors, their friends, who never came. "We waited all night," the husband said, his voice trembling as if the memory itself was too much to bear. His wife sat beside him, her hand gripping his, her silence speaking volumes. Their home was gone, swallowed by the earth, along with everyone they knew. The weight of their loss pressed into every word they spoke, grief and guilt twisting their voices into fragile echoes of the people they had once been.

These stories were fragments of a larger, darker whole—a tragedy that could never fully surface. Wayanad's misty hills had buried more than just lives; they had buried truths. Truths that no one wanted to confront. And as I listened, as I pieced together the suffering that still lived in the hearts of the survivors, I realized that this was only the tip of the iceberg. The landslide was not just a natural disaster. It had become a festering wound, left untreated by those who could have brought healing.

The contractors and officials who had overseen the recovery, the ones who had rushed to sweep the tragedy under the rug—they were the true architects of this ongoing nightmare. They had hushed the voices of the victims, covered up the truth to protect their profits, to avoid scandal. The land itself had been tainted, made unsellable by their denial, their greed. And in doing so, they had trapped the spirits, left them abandoned, bound in darkness.

With my eyes closed, I could see it clearly now. This wasn't just about hauntings or restless spirits. This was about justice. These spirits were not lost souls wandering aimlessly—they were enraged. Their fury was palpable, their pain tied to the lies and silence that had kept them hidden. They demanded recognition, demanded to be seen, to be heard. They had been wronged in life and in death, and the supernatural disturbances were nothing less than their way of forcing us to confront the truth we had tried to ignore.

The disturbances weren't random—they were the dead, demanding what had been stolen from them. And now it was my burden to uncover what lay hidden beneath Wayanad's misty hills, to bring the truth into the light, no matter how dark it might be.

With every new story that crossed my path, with every fragile document unearthed from the dusty archives, I felt the urgency building inside me. It was as though the voices in my head were growing louder, insistent, urging me to dig deeper, to uncover the buried truths before the land itself swallowed them back into darkness. The past was on the edge of vanishing again, and I could feel time working against me.

The next day, I stood at the door of Mrs. Menon's cottage, the woman whose name had lingered in the air like a whispered secret. She was said to be part of the very fabric of Wayanad, a woman who had lived through its joys and sorrows, who seemed as much a part of the land as the trees and the rain. Her small cottage, tucked away beneath the shade of oak trees that had seen more than a lifetime, stood as a living relic—untouched by modernity, yet bearing the weight of history.

The inside of her home was dense with the scent of old books, dried flowers, and something else—something intangible, like the essence of forgotten stories hovering just beyond reach. A single lamp flickered softly, casting an amber glow that lent the space a warmth, as though trying to preserve the past. There was a sense of time here, but not the relentless kind that marched forward. This time was cyclical, always circling back, folding in on itself, seeking solace in memories.

Mrs. Menon, delicate but strong in the way only the elderly seem to master, greeted me with eyes that knew more than they revealed and a smile that seemed to have traveled from another era. Her silver hair, braided neatly into a bun, gleamed in the soft light as she poured me tea—herbal, with a hint of jasmine that carried the scent of the wild garden beyond her door.

For a long time, we didn't speak. We didn't need to. The silence between us was thick with meaning, pregnant with the stories waiting to be told. It was Mrs. Menon who finally broke the quiet, her voice slow and deliberate, as though each word carried the weight of a lifetime. "The land itself cried out that night," she began, her eyes distant, locked on some far-off memory. "I swear on it. It wasn't just the earth shaking—there was something more. Something deeper."

I sat, captivated, as she spoke. Mrs. Menon told me of Wayanad as it once was, full of life and movement, its streets bustling with people, its shops alive with the rhythms of daily existence. But that night, the night the earth gave way, something changed forever. "It wasn't just the quaking of the ground," she continued, her voice a slow unraveling of old grief. "It was the voices. We heard them—the cries for help. And they never really stopped, did they?"

I could almost see it—Wayanad before the tragedy, vibrant, alive. But now, there was only the ghost of what once had been, and Mrs. Menon's words painted the picture with sharp, aching clarity. The land had been tampered with, corrupted by greed and ignorance. The recovery efforts had been rushed, the authorities overwhelmed and unwilling to face the full extent of the disaster. But deeper still, hidden beneath the surface of everything, was something far darker—a truth no one dared to speak aloud.

As Mrs. Menon shared detail after detail, the story I had been piecing together sharpened into focus. The land wasn't just haunted by restless spirits; it had been stained, corrupted by the weight of lives lost without meaning. The souls who cried out for help that night hadn't found peace, not because of some ancient curse, but because their lives had been erased, their deaths reduced to an inconvenience. And the land, now restless and broken, had become a prison for their spirits.

When Mrs. Menon finally stopped speaking, her eyes distant and glazed, I knew she had said all she could. There was no way to capture the full depth of her pain with words alone, but what she had given me was enough. I thanked her, my heart heavy with the burden of what I now knew, and as I turned to leave, she stopped me.

"Be careful, child," she whispered, her voice soft and full of a mother's pleading. "The land remembers. It always does."

As I left her cottage, her whispered blessing—a prayer for safety—echoed in my ears. I knew then that this journey was no longer just about uncovering the truth. It was about confronting the land itself, the very forces that had woven their way into the soil, into the air. And I would need all the strength I could find to face what lay ahead.

The next day, another piece of the puzzle fell into place, but this time it came from Ramesh—a former construction worker whose very presence seemed to sag under the weight of his untold secrets. I met him in a dimly lit cafe on the outskirts of town, far enough from the heart of

Wayanad to escape the immediate shadow of the hills, yet close enough to still feel their looming presence. The cafe had the air of a forgotten memory, with its dark wood, the low hum of flickering lights, and the shadows that stretched just long enough to hide guilt and shame.

Ramesh sat across from me, a husk of the man he must have once been. His shoulders slumped, his eyes hollowed by years of labor and something darker—something gnawing at him from the inside. He was reluctant to speak at first, his voice thick with the weight of the memories he'd tried to bury. But I pressed, and eventually, his resolve cracked, words slipping out like stones being pushed from a collapsing wall.

"Strange things..." he muttered, his voice low and dragging, as if dredging up each word from the depths of his soul. "The things you don't talk about. The things that can drive a man mad if he lets them get too close."

He described the long nights of impossible labor after the landslide. They worked tirelessly, clearing the debris, pushing themselves further into the darkness with every shift. But it wasn't long before the night-shift workers refused their assignments—men who had worked their whole lives in harsh conditions, men who never backed down, now swearing they had seen things that couldn't be explained. Shadows that moved at the edge of their vision, shapes that dissolved into nothing when the lights hit them. Debris that shifted, almost deliberately, as if guided by unseen hands. And the voices—at first just whispers, indistinct, but then later, cries, desperate and disembodied, echoing through the stillness of the night.

I could feel the tremble in Ramesh's voice as he recounted these moments, his fear so palpable that it almost seeped into me, as though by speaking the words, he was transferring some of his own terror. "The higher-ups hushed us," he said, his tone turning bitter. "Bad press, they said. Told us to keep it together, not to listen to nonsense."

But it wasn't nonsense. Not when the shadows seemed to have a life of their own, not when the land itself felt alive, malevolent. Not after workers started disappearing, one by one, without explanation. "It was like the land was breathing them in," Ramesh said, his eyes narrowing, as though even now he was afraid of what he had seen. "Like it wanted them. Wanted revenge."

He stared into the depths of his coffee, his hands shaking ever so slightly as he continued. "I saw it, you know... not just the shadows or the voices. I saw it in the land itself, the way it shifted. Like it was writhing in pain. Suffering. And it wanted us to feel it too."

His words hung in the air, heavy and unsettling. There was no doubt in my mind now—the land itself was alive with the pain of the past. It wasn't just haunted by restless spirits; it was driven by something deeper, something primal and furious. Ramesh's testimony only confirmed what I had been suspecting all along: the land wasn't just cursed—it was demanding something. And it wouldn't rest until it was acknowledged.

As I left the cafe, the weight of Ramesh's story pressed down on me like the very shadows he described. The truth of Wayanad's past was darker than I had imagined, and I was only beginning to scratch the surface.

A cold tremor rippled down my spine as the truth became clearer. The spirits weren't merely haunting; they were enforcing justice. Their cries, which echoed through the night, weren't aimless—they were a call for recognition, for someone to see the injustices that had chained them to this land. They were crying out for anyone who dared to listen.

Later, while combing through a stack of old belongings retrieved from the archives, I stumbled upon what felt like the ultimate testimony—a worn diary, its pages fragile from time, belonging to a name that had been all but forgotten: Rithika Nair.

As I opened the cover and began reading, Rithika's words were crisp, professional, the tone of a hard-nosed journalist chasing down a story. But as I turned each page, the clarity frayed. Her entries grew personal, raw, tinged with fear. What started as a promising investigation into the landslide's aftermath soon devolved into warnings—words meant to caution those who would follow in her footsteps. She had uncovered more than she could handle. An evil had seeped from the earth itself, she wrote, an evil compounded by the people who had buried the truth beneath lies.

And then I found the entry that would haunt me, the one where Rithika's steady script turned jagged and wild, as if her very sanity was slipping through her fingers:

"The spirits are not at peace. They are trapped, bound to this land by the injustice done to them. Their cries grow louder each night, their presence more forceful... The truth about the landslide is buried beneath layers of deceit. The land itself holds the key to their liberation. But beware—those who seek the truth must be prepared to face the darkness that lies at the heart of it all."

I felt a chill wrap itself around me, settling deep into my bones as I closed the diary, my hands trembling. Rithika had been here before me. She had uncovered the same darkness, had walked the same path, and yet... she had vanished. Whatever she had found, whatever evil had ensnared her, was powerful enough to erase her completely.

The burden of her unfinished work now fell on me. The land's pain—the pain Rithika had uncovered—was now mine to bear.

Wayanad was no ordinary place. It was a living memory, an entity stitched together by broken promises and forgotten oaths. The spirits weren't just aimless wanderers—they were guardians of something far worse, something older than the disaster that had torn their lives apart. The evil wasn't confined to the surface. It ran deep, deeper than any grave.

The finality of the diary's last page echoed through the silence as I shut the cover. It was a sound that seemed to mark the beginning of my descent into the heart of Wayanad's darkness. There was no turning back now. There was no redemption without confronting what lay beneath the earth—what had remained buried for far too long.

This wasn't just a journey anymore. It was a calling, a duty. I had to finish what Rithika had started. I had to uncover the truth, drag it into the light, and break the cursed bond that held the spirits captive in their eternal unrest. The guilty had to be unmasked, and the land that had been twisted by greed, death, and suffering needed to be reconciled with those it had consumed.

The shadows tugging at me from the depths of Wayanad would have their reckoning. My resolve hardened as I realized what lay ahead—danger, yes, but also the possibility of finally bringing peace to a place that had known only darkness. It was only by walking into the heart of that darkness that I could hope to bring the light back, not just for the dead, but for the living who had suffered in its shadow for so long.

VII
Shadows of the Past

I couldn't shake the chill that had settled into my bones since finding Rithika Nair's diary. Her words, so frantic, so desperate, echoed in my mind. The spirits weren't just restless—they were demanding something. Recognition, justice, something buried deeper than any grave. I felt it too. The truth I sought was more than hidden. It was actively being suppressed, and I knew the dangers that awaited if I ventured too far.

But I had to keep going.

The next morning, a heavy mist clung to the hills of Wayanad as I made my way to Lakshman's house. He had spent his life in the quiet corridors of government, with knowledge of Wayanad's troubled history running deeper than most. His home stood at the forest's edge, where the trees seemed to press in like silent watchers, their leaves thick with secrets.

When Lakshman opened the door, his stern eyes were already filled with questions. As I told him about the spirits and the landslide, the concern deepened across his weathered face. He led me to a dimly lit study, its walls lined with the history most would rather forget, and handed me a weathered map, his fingers lingering on the edges as if unwilling to release it.

"This land... it's cursed, Aadhira," Lakshman said quietly. "Long before the landslide, there were ancient burial grounds here. When the developers desecrated the land, they woke something vengeful."

I felt my heart tighten as he pulled out old documents—letters, warnings, records of deaths that went unacknowledged. One letter, brittle with age, predicted the landslide as the land's vengeance. A cold realization crept over me—this disaster hadn't been natural. It was retribution.

"Be careful," Lakshman warned, his voice grave. "Those responsible will go to any lengths to keep the truth buried."

I nodded, but I already knew that I was too deep to stop now.

Later, I found myself in the Wayanad library, its dusty archives hiding more than just books. Keshav, the librarian, gave me a knowing look as he slid old records across the table, his silence speaking volumes. As I combed through the papers, a web of corruption emerged, its threads all leading back to one man: Ravi Verma. His name appeared again and again—attached to permits, land deals, and whispered bribes. He had profited from the land, from the tragedy, and from the ghosts still lingering in the soil.

I had no choice. I had to confront him.

Ravi Verma's estate loomed over Wayanad like a fortress—an island of wealth amidst an ocean of decay. The wrought-iron gates slammed shut behind me with a foreboding clang, and as I walked down the winding driveway, the scent of jasmine twisted with the acrid stench of rot, hanging heavy in the air. The mansion stood before me, its modern structure clashing with traditional Kerala architecture in a way that felt wrong, as if even the house knew it didn't belong.

The silence was suffocating, broken only by the occasional creak of the trees swaying under their weight of secrets. The air grew colder as I approached the grand door, its carvings of gods and demons battling eternally. I hesitated before pressing the doorbell, its chime unnervingly clear in the stillness, cutting through the silence like a blade.

A man in a tailored suit answered the door, his eyes as cold as the stone beneath my feet. "Yes? What business do you have?" His voice was polished, controlled.

"I'm here to see Mr. Verma," I replied, surprised at the steadiness of my voice. "I need to speak with him personally."

His gaze flickered with something unreadable before he stepped aside, allowing me to enter. The door shut behind me with a finality that made my skin prickle.

The mansion's interior was suffocating in its wealth—polished marble floors, golden tapestries, and a grand staircase that seemed absurd in its opulence. Yet beneath all of it, I could feel the dread, thick like a fog that clung to the walls, seeping from the foundation. This wasn't a home. It was a monument to greed and power, built atop the bones of the forgotten.

The man returned after what felt like hours. "Mr. Verma will see you now."

He led me down an endless corridor until we arrived at a dark, heavy door. The room beyond was a study, grand yet sterile. A mahogany desk sat before tall windows that let in the last of the setting sun, painting the room in hues of red and gold. But there was no warmth here. Only shadows.

Ravi Verma sat behind the desk, his presence commanding but cold. His hair, greyed at the temples, only seemed to sharpen his calculated appearance. He was a man who knew control, who wielded power like a weapon.

"Ms. Aadhira," he said smoothly, his voice a dangerous blend of charm and menace. "Please, sit."

I complied, though every instinct screamed at me to leave. "I'm sure you're aware of the ramifications of the spirits tied to the land," I began, keeping my tone even. "They are restless, seeking justice for what was done to them."

His eyes flickered with irritation, though his smile never wavered. "Ms. Aadhira, folklore and superstition have a way of spiraling out of control. The landslide was a natural disaster. Nothing more."

I met his gaze, unwavering. "There's nothing natural about what happened. The land was desecrated. Lives were stolen, and those spirits won't rest until they are acknowledged."

The room seemed to grow darker, the air thicker than Verma's smile faded into something more dangerous. "You're playing a dangerous game," he warned, his voice a low growl. "The past is best left buried."

I leaned forward, meeting his cold eyes with every ounce of strength I had. "The dead have paid for your sins. If you think you can scare me into silence, you're wrong."

For a moment, neither of us moved. Then, slowly, a smile crept across his face—not one of amusement, but of a predator toying with its prey. "So be it," he said, rising from his desk. "But understand… the truth comes at a cost."

He moved to a bookshelf and pulled down a large, worn tome. The leather-bound book thudded onto the desk, its weight vibrating through the room. "If you're so eager to find the truth, start here. But know this—once you open it, there is no turning back."

My fingers trembled as I reached for the book, its cover cold beneath my touch. When I opened it, the pages revealed images I didn't understand, symbols that twisted in the dim light. Faces lost in eternal torment stared back at me from the pages, and ancient rites were scrawled in a language I couldn't decipher.

As I read, my heart pounded in my chest. This wasn't just a curse. The land had been deliberately defiled. The spirits weren't simply restless—they were prisoners, trapped by something dark, something far older than any of us had realized.

Verma watched me with a dark satisfaction as he spoke, his voice low and sinister. "You think you can uncover the past without consequence, Ms. Aadhira? Every key requires a sacrifice."

I stared at the book, the weight of the truth crushing down on me. Whatever I was about to uncover, it would change everything. But I couldn't turn back now. The spirits needed to be freed, and I was the only one left to do it.

With my hands clenched around the cursed tome, I steeled myself for what was to come.

VIII
The Hidden Truth

The documents I'd taken from Ravi Verma's estate consumed my days and sleepless nights. Each weathered page I turned peeled back more layers of the sinister history buried beneath Wayanad, revealing a twisted web of corruption, desecration, and malevolent forces that had festered beneath the land for decades. The tragedy of the landslide, it seemed, was no act of nature. It resulted from greed—human arrogance that had defied and enraged the spirits that had once rested beneath the soil.

Among the papers, one journal stood out. The handwriting—frantic and hurried—belonged to an engineer named Dev. His early entries were mundane, documenting the progress of the construction, the typical setbacks of any large-scale project. But as I read deeper, the tone shifted. What started as frustration with logistics transformed into something darker, filled with an increasing sense of dread.

The workers had uncovered ancient burial sites—what they initially thought were merely rock formations. But soon, the bones appeared, weathered and fragile, unmistakably human. The workers knew. The land had been disturbed, and they had awakened something sacred. Yet, out of fear of their overseer, they pressed on.

Dev's journal detailed the moment they discovered the first remains. The machinery ground to a halt as if the earth itself resisted their intrusion. The workers were horrified, steeped in the traditions of their ancestors, and pleaded to stop the digging. They wanted to perform a small ritual to honor the dead. But when Ravi Verma arrived, there was no sympathy in his cold eyes. He didn't care about bones, rituals, or the sacredness of the land. To him, it was just another delay—another cost. He laughed off the workers' fears, dismissing them as backward superstitions.

The journal's tone became more frantic as Dev wrote of the escalating strangeness. The workers were on edge, some refusing to continue. Shadows moved at the edge of the floodlights, only to vanish when looked at directly. Tools disappeared, machinery malfunctioned without cause, and the air was filled with a low, oppressive hum, as if the very ground were whispering warnings.

There was one night that chilled me to the core. Dev had stayed late at the site, finishing paperwork. Alone in the dark, an icy dread crept over him as the sensation of being watched grew unbearable. He looked up and saw a figure—a shadow — standing just beyond the reach of the lights. It didn't move. It simply watched. Dev approached, but with every step, the figure seemed to fade, dissolving into the night air, leaving behind only a bone-deep chill.

Dev's entries grew desperate. Workers fell ill, with no explanation. Equipment failures became dangerous, almost deliberate. The land itself seemed to rebel. Dev had pleaded with Verma to stop, but the tycoon's response was chilling. He ordered the remains reburied in an unmarked grave, hidden beneath layers of concrete and steel. The workers, under Verma's command, were forced to bury the past without ceremony, silencing the dead.

The last entries were nearly illegible, the words smeared and trembling. Dev spoke of shadowy figures that appeared more frequently, always just out of reach. The workers were terrified. Illness spread, the equipment continued to fail, and the figures—they were no longer content to linger at the edges. Dev wrote of an overwhelming sense that they had awoken something ancient, something furious that would not rest until justice was served. He knew he had been complicit in the desecration. His final entry spoke of his intention to go to the authorities, to expose everything. But the entry was never finished, the sentence trailing off into nothingness.

Dev had disappeared. Vanished. And I was left with more questions than answers. What had happened to him? Had Verma silenced him, as he had the workers, before he could reveal the full extent of the horror beneath Wayanad? And more disturbingly, how was I supposed to pacify spirits that had been so grievously wronged?

I closed the journal, my hands trembling. The weight of Dev's words settled heavily on me. I could feel the urgency in his final thoughts. The spirits weren't just restless—they were demanding justice. Ravi Verma had desecrated the land, and in doing so, he had stirred something that would not be contained. The landslide had been the first strike, the spirits' fury bursting through the earth. But it wouldn't be the last.

The next morning, journal in hand, I went to the local police station. An aging officer listened as I recounted Dev's words, his face grim as I revealed the buried bones, the apparitions, and the shadowy figures stalking the land. He didn't seem surprised. He said little, but his warning was clear: Dev had pushed too far. His disappearance had been hushed up, and no one had been willing to question it.

I left the station with a growing sense of dread. Dev's fate had been sealed the moment he challenged Verma. But I couldn't stop now. Too much had already been revealed. I needed more answers, and there was only one person left who might have them.

I found Ramesh in the same dim cafe where we had met before. He looked even more worn down than the last time, his eyes heavy with exhaustion and fear. He confirmed Dev's fears—there was something deeply wrong with the land, and Verma had been involved in more than just a cover-up. Ramesh pointed me to Murali, a former foreman who had worked the site until the night of the landslide.

Murali lived in a grim, shuttered house on the outskirts of town. His eyes were hollow, his voice thin as he spoke. After Verma had ordered the remains reburied, everything had gone wrong. Workers had fallen ill, the land had rebelled, and the spirits—those shadowy figures—had become more than just specters. They had become a force, angry and vengeful. Dev had planned to reveal everything, but before he could act, he had vanished.

Murali's words left no doubt in my mind. Verma had buried more than bones. He had buried the truth. And now, the spirits wouldn't rest until justice had been served. This wasn't just about acknowledging the dead—it was about making right the grievous wrongs that had been done.

With time running out and the spirits' fury growing, I knew what I had to do. I needed undeniable proof. Proof that could dismantle Verma's empire and bring peace to the restless spirits of Wayanad. The cost would be high. But I had no choice. The truth had to come out.

IX

Buried Truths

I spent the next few days locked in an obsession, my mind feverish with the weight of what I'd uncovered. Each piece of evidence seemed to hum with urgency, and with each turn of the page, the enormity of Ravi Verma's crimes became clearer. This wasn't just about exposing a corrupt businessman; it was about freeing the souls trapped in this land, desperate for justice.

The construction site—where Verma had ordered the bones of the forgotten to be buried in secret—loomed in my thoughts like a festering wound. The place was abandoned now, left to nature's creeping vines and soil, but for me, it held the key to everything. It was where I had to go next, no matter the danger. But I couldn't do this alone.

I went to Prasanna, knowing she would understand the gravity of what I needed to ask. Her kitchen was a monument to loss, the walls lined with photographs that reminded her daily of a life torn apart. The faint smell of spices lingered in the air, but nothing could mask the scent of grief.

Her eyes met mine as I entered. They were hollow, darkened by sleepless nights and the weight of too many unanswered questions. "Aadhira," she whispered, her voice thin and brittle. "What is it?"

Across from her, I hesitated, unsure if I was prepared to involve her in this nightmare again. "I need your help, Prasanna. I've found things—evidence that could finally bring Verma down, but we need more. It's at the site, buried with those remains. If we find something concrete, we can finally put this to rest. The spirits, the injustice... everything."

Her hands trembled as she clutched the edge of the table. "After all this time, you think something's still there?"

That is correct, I do. I know it's dangerous, but I can't do this without you. I need your strength.

For a moment, her face softened, almost as if hope dared to flicker in the dark recesses of her mind. Then it hardened. "If this is what it takes to stop him, to give my family peace... then I'm with you."

With Prasanna on my side, I knew I could gather others. I reached out to Raghav next, meeting him in a secluded tea shop on the outskirts of town. The mist clung to the hills outside, wrapping the world in an eerie silence. His eyes, red-rimmed and weary, met mine over the steam of his tea.

"Raghav, we're going back to the site. We need more evidence—something solid to expose Verma. I know you've seen things too. I could use your help."

His hands shook slightly as he lifted the cup to his lips, the weight of what he'd seen etched into every line on his face. "I've been haunted by shadows since that night," he murmured, his voice low and haunted. "If the spirits want the truth to come out, I'll help. I can't live like this anymore."

A sense of relief washed over me as Raghav's words settled. "We need to be quiet about this. Verma can't know we're coming."

He nodded, his gaze steady despite the tremor in his hands. "I'm ready."

Together, we gathered more allies, each one haunted by the same disturbances that had plagued our town. Mrs. Suresh, a retired schoolteacher, was the last to join us. Her home, meticulous and orderly, betrayed no sign of the turmoil that had invaded her life.

"I've felt them too," she said, her voice trembling as she folded her hands in her lap. "The cold drafts, the books falling off the shelves for no reason. The spirits want to be heard, Aadhira. If this helps them find peace, I'm in."

That evening, we gathered in Prasanna's living room, a small group united by the horrors we had faced. The air hummed with anticipation, thick with unspoken fear. I spread a map of the construction site across the coffee table, marking the spots we believed held the key to unlocking the truth.

Silence hung heavily in the room until Prasanna finally spoke. "If we find what we're looking for, how do we bring it to light? Verma has power—he'll bury this if he can."

I looked her square in the eye, my voice firm. "Once we have the evidence, I'll take it to a journalist, someone outside of Verma's reach. We need to expose him, and we need to do it right."

Raghav clenched his fists, his jaw tight. "We've been living in fear for too long. We can't let him win."

Mrs. Suresh nodded, her face solemn. "The spirits have chosen us. We must tread carefully, but this cannot be left unfinished."

In that moment, something shifted. It wasn't just resolve—it was a shared understanding. We were no longer individuals weighed down by fear. We were a force, bound by the same purpose: to expose the truth, free the spirits, and finally bring Ravi Verma to justice.

What we were about to do was dangerous. We knew that. But the time for fear had passed. There was no turning back now. We were ready to face whatever the darkness had in store for us.

The night swallowed us whole, the overgrown wilderness of the abandoned construction site looming like a graveyard forgotten by time. The rusted machinery, left to decay, jutted out of the earth like the skeletons of failed ambition, their purpose long extinguished. We moved quietly, our footsteps muted by the soft soil, navigating through a maze of weeds and crumbling structures. The air felt thick, oppressive, like it was pressing down on us, weighing each breath.

Something in the silence felt wrong. It wasn't just the absence of sound—it was something else. The darkness felt alive, pulsating with a malevolence I couldn't shake. Even the trees, gnarled, seemed to lean toward us, their branches reaching out like skeletal hands, trying to pull us deeper into their embrace.

Each step we took felt heavier, like we were being drawn into another world. Shadows flickered at the edges of our vision, moving in ways that defied logic. The temperature dipped without warning, and I could feel it—an icy breath against the back of my neck, as if something unseen was watching, waiting. Every instinct told me to turn back, but we had come too far.

We finally reached the first marked spot on the map. Without a word, we began digging, the sound of metal scraping against soil filling the air like a dirge. The earth resisted us, clinging to its secrets, refusing to give them up easily. With every shovelful of dirt, the oppressive energy around us thickened, and the feeling of being watched became unbearable. The spirits, I realized, were gathering. Their anger and sorrow pulsed in the air, wrapping around us.

Hours passed in silence, broken only by the rhythmic sound of digging. Then, the shovel struck something hard—a dull, metallic thud that froze us in place. We crouched down, hands trembling, and began brushing the dirt away. What we uncovered was worse than we had imagined.

A mass grave, bodies tangled together in death, their remains in varying stages of decay. The sight of human bones, disjointed and intertwined, sent a wave of nausea through me. The hollow sockets of skulls stared up at us, pleading for release from their torment. My breath caught in my throat, and I had to force myself to keep moving. Beside me, Prasanna's breaths were shallow, each one strained under the weight of the horror we had unearthed.

Then, something caught the faint light of our lanterns—a small, rusted metal box buried beneath the bones. My hands, shaking with a mixture of fear and urgency, worked quickly to unearth it. The latch was corroded, barely holding together, but with a hard pull, it gave way, and the lid creaked open.

Inside were relics of the past—documents, contracts, letters—all stained with age but unmistakably incriminating. The signatures of Ravi Verma and his associates were clear, their crimes hidden beneath layers of deceit. The papers were littered with annotations in red ink, marking cover-ups, bribes, and the deliberate erasure of the burial sites. And then there were the photographs—workers, pale-faced and grim, standing at the very site where we now crouched, unaware they were documenting their own doom.

But the last item, a journal, was what chilled me to my core. The leather-bound cover cracked as I opened it, the pages brittle with age. The handwriting inside was frantic, scrawled in a rush. It belonged to Rajiv, one of Verma's engineers. As the pages turned, his earlier entries, which were mundane and filled with details of the project, took on a different tone. His excitement turned to fear as they uncovered the burial sites. His warnings were clear—Verma had known what they had found but ordered the remains to be reburied, silencing the workers with threats. Rajiv had sensed the growing unease, the spirits stirring beneath the earth, their anger rising.

One line stood out, etched into the paper as if written in a moment of panic: "Something was stirred when we disturbed those graves—something that won't let us rest."

I felt the weight of Rajiv's last words pressing down on me. He had buried the journal, knowing the truth might never come to light. His words, his fear, and the spirits he wrote of—they were all too real.

"What is it?" Prasanna's voice broke the silence, her words trembling.

"This," I said, clutching the journal tightly, "is what we need to expose Verma. But there's more here. The spirits won't rest until we uncover everything."

The surrounding air shifted. The cold deepened, and I could hear them now—the voices. Low, mournful, filled with anguish. The wind seemed to carry their pain, wrapping it around us. The ground beneath our feet trembled, a subtle movement that sent chills down my spine.

"We need to leave," I urged, the weight of the spirits' presence pressing in on us. But before we could move, the metallic clang of a gate echoed behind us, a sound that reverberated through the still night.

A shadow detached itself from the darkness. It wasn't human—it was twisted, malformed, its features barely discernible. Its hollow eyes bore into us, filled with rage and sorrow, a grotesque witness to the atrocities buried beneath the ground.

A scream tore through the night, a sound so raw and piercing it felt like it was ripping through my very soul. The spirit moved closer, feeding off our fear, its presence suffocating.

"Hurry—move!" I shouted, pushing Prasanna forward as the others scrambled to their feet. We ran, the shadows clawing at our heels, the malevolence of the land pulling us back.

As the trees closed in around us, their branches reached out like claws. The air grew thicker, heavier, until it felt like we were drowning in it. The light from our lanterns flickered, threatening to go out entirely, and for a moment, I thought we wouldn't make it.

But then, just as the shadows closed in, we broke through the trees, the first light of dawn breaking through the horizon. We collapsed onto the grass, breathless and trembling, but alive. The evidence, clutched tightly in my arms, was our only hope now.

The spirits wouldn't stop. Not until the truth was revealed. But I knew we had only scratched the surface. The darkness that clung to Wayanad ran deeper than any of us had imagined, and what we had found tonight was only the beginning.

&

As dawn broke across the horizon, streaks of red and orange bleeding into the sky, I stared at the screen, waiting for Suresh's reply. The email I'd just sent felt like I'd unleashed something unstoppable—words that had the power to topple empires, break apart lives, and expose a darkness that had been buried for too long.

The rusted box sat on the table beside me, its grim contents staring back like the ghosts of those we couldn't save. I couldn't stop running my fingers over the lid, the rough edges biting into my skin as if trying to remind me of the weight of what we'd uncovered. This wasn't just about spirits anymore—this was about men like Ravi Verma who thought they could rewrite history to suit their greed, burying lives beneath the earth along with their sins.

I had to keep moving, had to act while the world still spun in our favor. The thought of the evidence falling into the wrong hands made my chest tighten. We were playing with fire now, and Verma had the resources to extinguish it before we could even get close to the truth.

The box, the documents, the photographs—all of it needed to be sent out before the tendrils of his influence could reach us. Suresh had contacts, people who could spread the story like wildfire. Once the truth was out, once the world knew what had happened on that cursed land, not even Verma could silence it.

But every second that ticked by felt like a step closer to danger. I could almost feel the spirits stirring around us, waiting—no, demanding—that we finish what we'd started. They had waited long enough for justice. Their voices, once whispers in the night, had grown louder, more insistent, as if urging me forward.

I let out a breath I hadn't realized I'd been holding. He was right. The forces we'd uncovered weren't just men like Verma—they were the spirits of the land, angry and unforgiving. We were caught in the middle, between the living and the dead, between justice and corruption. But we were. No turning back now.

I stood, the rusted box heavy in my arms. The secrets inside felt like they were burning through the metal, their truth too powerful to be contained. I had planned to mail it the next day, in the chaos of daylight, but now the urgency hummed in my veins. I couldn't wait. Every moment was a gamble, and I wasn't willing to bet on time.

The package needed to be delivered now, under the veil of dawn, when the world was still waking, and the shadows hadn't yet caught up to us. I grabbed the papers, the journal, and the photographs, packing them with care, knowing they were our only weapons against Verma's empire.

This wasn't just about ghosts anymore. This was about justice—for the dead and for the living. I would let no one silence them again.

Suresh

In a world where truth was constantly twisted, I had always held on to one principle—integrity. It was that value that connected me to Suresh, a man who understood the weight of truth as much as I did. We met years ago, under circumstances neither of us could have expected, but it was in that chaos that our bond was forged. And that bond has been unshakable ever since.

Back then, I wasn't the investigator I've become. While working as a cybersecurity analyst in Bengaluru, I was still discovering the inner workings of the world. I was in the middle of a scandal—company data had been breached, a breach with the potential to ruin lives. I was tasked with figuring out what had happened and how deep the problem went. What I found was more than I had bargained for—a web of corruption, hidden behind the breach, waiting to destroy anyone who got too close.

That's when Suresh appeared. He worked for a major newspaper, and his reputation preceded him. Unlike the other reporters, he was different. No, Suresh had a gift. He could take raw data and turn it into a story that mattered, one that made people sit up and take notice. Rather than simply exposing the facts, he gave them a human touch. He made people care about the injustices behind the numbers.

At first, I didn't trust him. I wasn't sure if he was one of those reporters who would sensationalize the story and leave us to clean up the mess. But the more we spoke, the more I realized we were after the same thing. Justice. Truth. The stories no one wanted to tell because they were too ugly, too real.

Together, we uncovered the corruption that had been buried beneath the surface, and with Suresh's reporting, the world saw it too. His articles didn't just inform; they forced action. They pushed people in power to face accountability, to answer for their sins. And somewhere in the middle of all that chaos, I knew I could trust him. Not just as a journalist, but as someone who believed in the fight for truth as much as I did.

Over time, we became a team. While I worked in the shadows, gathering the evidence no one else could see, Suresh turned those details into narratives that held power.

He gave life to the stories that needed to be told, and his words created ripples that turned into waves. Together, we brought corrupt officials to justice and exposed lies that no one else dared touch.

Now, with the weight of Wayanad's ghosts pressing down on me, there was no one else I could turn to. Suresh was the only one who would understand the gravity of what we were dealing with—the corruption, the desecration of the land, and the restless spirits trapped by greed and deceit. I hadn't spoken to him in months, but I knew his moral compass hadn't shifted. He was the one person who could take this story, this truth, and make sure it realized.

The evidence I held—the documents, the photographs, the journal—was explosive, and it wasn't just about bringing down Ravi Verma. This was about justice for the forgotten, for the spirits that refused to be silenced. Suresh would know how to handle it. He'd cut through the lies like a blade, sharp and unrelenting, and bring the truth to the surface.

I didn't have to second-guess my decision. In the dark, tangled mess of Wayanad, where shadows whispered of horrors yet to be uncovered, I knew Suresh was my best hope. Perhaps my only hope. Together, we'd bring justice—not just for the living, but for the dead too.

৪১

The morning air felt wrong. There was no warmth, no comfort in the rising sun. The cars refused to start, as if the engines knew something we didn't. My phone was dead, the signal unreachable, and the world seemed to contract, suffocating us beneath an unseen force. It was as if the land had closed itself off, trapping us here.

I glanced at the others. Prasanna, Raghav, and the rest stood close, their eyes darting nervously around the old house. The structure groaned, the timber creaking as if it had grown into a malignant spirit of its own. Shadows twisted at the corners of our vision, but every time we looked directly at them, they disappeared. The darkness was toying with us, daring us to acknowledge its presence.

We huddled near the flickering lantern, the only thing keeping the growing terror at bay. The light sputtered, struggling to stay alive, just like our hope. The air thickened, heavy with an unnatural weight, and I could feel the cold seep into my bones, making each breath feel like it was fighting through a layer of frost.

Then Prasanna's gaze caught something. Along the far wall, ink-black lines smeared across the wooden planks. We watched in horrified silence as the lines twisted and coalesced, forming words in a crude, spidery script. Below the haunting message, a rough map appeared, scratched into the ancient timber.

"Dig here—the truth lies deeper still."

My heart sank. I didn't want to say it, but I knew I had to. "They're leading us," I whispered, the words barely audible. "To where more is buried."

Raghav's voice cracked, the fear etched deep in his face. "But what about the evidence? You said you'd send it. We have enough to take Verma down."

I shook my head; the coldness settling into my chest. "We can't stop now. There's more they want us to find. We need everything. And then we send it."

It was clear, even if we didn't want to admit it—this wasn't over. Not by a long shot.

We gathered what we could and left Prasanna's house, feeling the weight of unseen eyes following us into the forest. The familiar path through the trees had become something else, something darker. The branches overhead no longer offered shelter; they caged us in, trapping us beneath their gnarled limbs.

The map led us to a clearing, the ground uneven and scarred from old excavation attempts. I felt the pull in my gut—the spirits wanted us here. The air was thick with tension, the kind that makes your skin prickle, warning you that you've gone too far. My instincts screamed to turn back, but I knew we couldn't. Not now.

We dug, the shovels slicing into the earth. With each movement, the ground seemed to resist, clinging to its secrets as if it knew what we were trying to unearth. The more we dug, the heavier the air became, until it felt like we were suffocating under the weight of something far older than us, something waiting to be found.

After what felt like hours, the shovel hit something solid. The sound echoed, sharp and foreboding. We knelt, hands trembling, and brushed away the dirt. What we uncovered stopped us cold.

A mass grave. Bones, tangled together, remnants of lives forgotten and buried in haste. The sight of those skeletal remains, half-buried, told a story of atrocity and neglect. Their hollow eyes stared back at us, pleading for an end to their suffering.

Beside me, Prasanna whispered, her voice trembling. "What have we done?"

We cleared more earth, and something metallic glinted beneath the bones. A rusted box, half-rotted by time. I pulled it free, my hands shaking as I forced the latch open. Inside were documents—evidence, contracts, letters, all signed by Verma and his associates. And with them, photographs. Faded, but clear enough to show the workers, the construction site, and the very place where we now stood.

But the most chilling discovery was the journal. Rajiv's journal. His words, scrawled in desperation, revealed the truth we had feared. Verma knew. He had always known. And he had buried the evidence—literally and figuratively—beneath layers of lies and dirt.

As I read Rajiv's last entry, the ground beneath us shifted. The earth groaned, and I felt it—a presence, ancient and angry, stirring below. We had disturbed something that didn't want to be found.

The temperature plummeted, and I heard it—a voice, mournful and filled with rage. "You disturbed us. Now you dig further than you can handle."

I froze. From the shadows, figures emerged, no longer just flickers at the edge of my vision. They stood before us, twisted remnants of the dead, their skeletal hands reaching out, their hollow eyes burning with fury. They had risen for one reason—to make us pay for the truth we had uncovered.

The cold wrapped around us, suffocating, and I knew we had crossed a line. The spirits weren't hiding anymore. They were here, fully realized, ready to claim justice for the sins committed against them.

I gripped the journal, my heart pounding. This wasn't just about evidence. This was about survival—ours and theirs. The dead had come for a reckoning, and we were the ones who had to deliver it.

I could feel the land beneath us shifting, cracking open, demanding everything. The truth we had sought was only the beginning. The price for uncovering it... was something none of us were prepared to pay.

X

The Final Revelation

The rhythmic thud of the shovels had been the only sound, a steady pulse breaking the otherwise suffocating quiet of the forest. Then it came—a light and silver, drifting into view like a forgotten memory surfacing from the depths of some ancient dream. It hovered, casting an ethereal glow over the trees, transforming them into looming, ghostly sentinels. The air shifted, thick with something unseen yet undeniably present. It wasn't just light—it was a presence, old and watchful, carrying with it the weight of centuries.

I felt my heart quicken, my breath hitching as I stared at the orb. "It's... trying to show us something," I whispered, more to myself than anyone else. Without warning, the words emerged, as if they didn't fully belong to me. The others exchanged uneasy glances, but none of us moved. The light pulsed, slow and deliberate, as though it were alive, waiting for us to understand. Then it floated deeper into the forest, beckoning us with an otherworldly invitation.

Without thinking, I followed. Suddenly, the forest closed in around us, its trees towering and their twisted branches clawing at the sky like something feral. The further we ventured, the more alive the forest felt—its breath mingled with ours, its roots seemed to pulse beneath the ground. The light led us through the tangled paths, slipping through the shadows as if it had always belonged to the dark. Each step brought the air thicker, denser, pressing on my lungs like the weight of forgotten truths.

My pulse echoed in my ears, a frantic beat that matched the rhythm of the orb's glow. I couldn't help but feel it—a strange, inexplicable connection. It was as if the light was pulling me toward something, dragging me into its world where reality and myth blurred. And yet, I kept going. We all did. Because once you've started following something like this, how do you turn back?

The deeper we went, the more treacherous the forest became. Thorny vines and underbrush snagged at our clothes, sharp branches sliced through the air like skeletal fingers. It was no longer a path—the twisted path had transformed into something else, a labyrinth specifically designed to ensnare us. The trees closed in, their gnarled limbs twisting overhead, blocking out the sky. The air hummed with a low, pulsating energy, as though the land itself was holding its breath, waiting for what came next.

Each rustle in the leaves, every distant creak of wood, sent a new wave of unease through me. The forest wasn't just alive—it was watching. Waiting. Despite that, the light continued, and so did we.

I tried to push the doubt from my mind, to focus on the chase, but it gnawed at me. What was this light? Why was it leading us? And where was it taking us? My life had always been about finding answers, untangling webs of lies and deceit, but this—this was different. Here, in the forest's thick, I wasn't chasing data or decrypting codes. I was chasing something far older, far darker. Something that had no rules, no logic.

The orb's glow reflected off the trees, casting long, sinister shadows that danced along the ground. And with each step, the pull grew stronger, more urgent. I felt it in my bones—this wasn't just about the truth. It was about something much bigger. Something ancient, buried deep within the forest and the earth beneath us.

The light flickered, as if pausing, before dipping low to the ground and halting just ahead. I stopped, the others gathering around me. The forest was still now, the air thick with tension. The orb hovered above a patch of earth, its glow soft but insistent.

Prasanna's voice broke the silence, trembling. "What... what does it want?"

I didn't answer. I already knew. It wanted us to dig. Just like before. But this time, it felt different. The earth seemed to pulse beneath our feet, alive with energy. This was no ordinary ground. There was something here—something buried, waiting to be uncovered.

I reached for the shovel, my hands shivering. The others watched in silence, their breaths shallow, their fear palpable. As I drove the shovel into the ground, the earth seemed to groan in response. Each dig felt heavier, as though the soil itself was resisting. But the light pulsed, urging us on.

The ground shifted beneath us, a low rumble vibrating through the earth. Something was down there, waiting to be unearthed. Something far more dangerous than we could have imagined.

My hands shook, but I couldn't afford to let fear take root. The crate felt heavy, its weight not just physical, but steeped in the gravity of whatever lay inside. I pried the lid open, the wood splintering under my grip, and the surrounding air seemed to shift—a tension snapping into place as if the very forest was holding its breath.

Inside the crate, nestled beneath layers of crumbling fabric, were artifacts that spoke of forgotten times. An old metal pendant glinted in the low light, its once-polished surface now tarnished. Papers, yellowed and brittle, lay stacked haphazardly, their ink faded but still legible. I reached for the topmost document, my fingers grazing the edge. As I lifted it, the faint scent of musty decay filled my nostrils.

The contents of the crate weren't just relics—they were records, letters, and journals. Each piece was a puzzle that, when put together, painted a far darker picture than I had expected. Names of people long dead, deals struck in shadows, and signatures belonging to the ones who had tried to bury the truth.

I felt the weight of it in my hands, the truth that had hidden in this forsaken forest for too long. "It's all here," I whispered, turning to the others, their wide-eyed expressions mirroring the realization that we were standing on the cusp of something monumental. The air felt thick with the spirits' presence, as if they were watching us, waiting for us to see what had been done to them, to their land.

Raghav, standing just behind me, exhaled sharply, his voice barely a rasp. "What is this?"

"Everything," I replied, voice steady despite the storm of emotions inside me. "This is the truth Verma didn't want anyone to find." My gaze dropped back to the documents—corruption, land theft, desecration. It was all here in black and white. The lives were stolen, not just by the landslide, but by the greed that had ripped apart this place long before the earth crumbled.

But as I sifted through the papers, my fingers brushing over an old journal, a cold sensation crept up my spine. The surrounding shadows deepened, thickening in a way that didn't feel natural. I glanced up. The forest seemed darker than it had just moments before. The oppressive silence pressed in harder, and I could feel it—the spirits. They were close, closer than ever before.

"We need to get out of here," Prasanna whispered, her voice taut with fear.

But I wasn't done. Not yet. There was more buried here, something deeper. I could feel it in my bones, an unspoken pull toward the ground beneath our feet. This wasn't just about the documents or the journal. The light had led us here for a reason, and I would not leave without knowing what it was.

I knelt down, brushing away the dirt still clinging to the base of the crate, my hands moving with a feverish urgency. And then, my fingers grazed something cold, metallic. A small latch, almost hidden beneath the earth. I yanked at it, feeling the catch give way with a soft click.

Beneath the crate was a false bottom, and tucked inside was a small, rusted box. I hesitated for only a moment before flipping the lid open. Inside was a single item—a pendant, delicate and intricate, the design unlike anything I'd ever seen. It hummed with a quiet energy, and the moment I touched it, I knew.

This was what the spirits wanted. This pendant held their pain, their rage. It was the key to everything.

As soon as my fingers closed around it, the ground beneath us rumbled, a low, menacing growl from the depths of the earth. The air thickened with an unnatural cold, and the forest seemed to come alive with a malevolent presence. The spirits weren't just watching—they were here.

The shadows shifted, and from the corner of my eye, I saw them. Figures, half-formed, flickering in and out of the darkness. Their eyes burned with something far beyond anger—pure, unbridled fury. They had waited too long, suffered too much, and now they wanted their justice.

"We need to go. Now." My voice came out tight, breathless, as the ground shuddered beneath us.

But I knew, even as we turned to leave, that this wasn't over. The truth was out, yes, but the spirits weren't done. They had been wronged, buried alive under lies and greed. And now, they were going to make sure everyone paid the price.

❧

Inside the crate, the gruesome reality of this land's dark history revealed itself to me. A heap of bones, decaying clothes, and shattered lives stared back, each fragment a silent monument to terror and loss. Forgotten souls, now mere remnants, lay there—unwept and unburied, trapped in the stony soil's embrace. The stench of death clawed its way up my throat, almost suffocating me.

I could barely breathe as I tore my eyes away from the macabre scene. Amidst the shattered bones and faded dreams, something caught my attention—documents pristine in a ruin that had swallowed everything else. My heart raced as I brushed the dirt from the papers. The file—it was familiar, even through the layers of grime and decay. I had seen it before, pristine and crisp, back when

Ravi Verma handed it to me in his bungalow.

Ravi Verma... his name echoed in my mind, now tainted with something darker than I had ever imagined. As I held the file, its weight felt unbearable. Not because of its physical heft, but because of what it symbolized. The sins, the secrets, had seeped into these pages. And I, unknowingly, had carried them all this time.

The realization hit me like a blow. This grisly collection of bones, these documents hidden among the dead—they held more than I had ever expected.

Ravi had known.

All this time, he had known what this file represented, and worse, he had relished it. His hands were stained with the blood of those whose remains now surrounded me. Divine justice? No. Something far darker had compelled him to bury it all here, mocking the very idea of retribution. And here I was, uncovering his secrets, long after I had been played like a pawn in his twisted game.

I gasped, the truth tightening around my throat like a noose. My fingers gripped the file, as if it were the only thing anchoring me to reality. But my mind was spiraling back, reliving every lie, every deceitful word Ravi had spoken. His calm tone, the measured smiles—everything had been a facade, hiding the evil lurking underneath. It was more than betrayal; it was a grotesque manipulation of trust, a web far beyond anything I had imagined.

I wanted to run. My heart screamed at me to flee, but my mind was trapped, overwhelmed by the flood of memories. I saw myself walking through the lavish halls of Verma's home. The wealth, the cold opulence—it all masked a deeper, malevolent intent. The polished floors, the heavy curtains, the elegant furniture—everything was a lie.

And then the pieces fell into place. I nearly collapsed under the weight of the realization. I had been ensnared in his game from the very beginning. The light, the forest, everything had conspired to bring me here, to this moment.

This wasn't an investigation. It was punishment—punishment for a crime I hadn't even known I was committing.

The memories sharpened, becoming painfully clear. I saw it all again, like a nightmare playing on repeat. Leaving Verma's house, file in hand, believing I was seeking justice. But then, the world tilted. Pain exploded through my skull as darkness consumed me.

I had died here. Not just figuratively—literally. My life had been ripped from me, my body discarded like so many others before me. I had fought for justice, only to be buried in the same forgotten grave. The cold, ultimate truth settled into my bones. The box—this cursed box I had uncovered—held not just Verma's skeletons.

It held mine.

My breath was ragged as I looked at the grave, the clearing that now felt like an epitaph. But something shifted in the air, and I noticed them—Prasanna, Raghav, my friends, my allies. They weren't just companions chasing the truth. They, too, had fallen victim to the same ruthless fate.

Their ghostly forms took shape, sorrow, and pain etched into every feature. My heart clenched, not from fear, but from the crushing understanding that we were the same. Trapped, tethered to this cursed place, unable to move on because of the way our lives had been desecrated.

Despite the agony in their eyes, their expressions softened. A strange calm passed through me, an unspoken understanding. We were all part of the same grim story, a chapter that had yet to close. And as they dissolved into the light, I felt it too—chains breaking, piece by piece.

The spirits drifted into the glow, their forms fading into the forest, taking with them the weight of their sorrow. I felt myself being pulled as well, toward a place beyond the physical world. The surrounding forest faded, and with it, the torment of the past. For the first time, I felt peace settling over me.

But just as I was ready to surrender to it, a voice cut through the silence. Familiar. Desperate.

"Aadhira!"

Dev. His voice reached through the mist, through the worlds I could no longer touch. I could feel his sorrow, his need to pull me back, but I couldn't respond. I was already moving beyond this world, leaving behind the haunted ghats of Wayanad and the terrible weight of what had been.

I was gone.

ॐ

Back in the living's world, I felt the ground beneath my feet unsteady as I stumbled out of Aadhira's house. My mind reeled with confusion, a weight pressing down on me. I had just been there with her—discussing the next steps, talking like nothing was wrong. But something was wrong. Deeply wrong. I couldn't shake the feeling that the edges of reality had blurred, slipping away into something I couldn't quite grasp.

There had been a strange coldness in her presence. I had brushed it off at first, but now it gnawed at me. Her movements were too fluid, too smooth—almost disconnected from the physical world. Her voice... it carried an echo, distant, like it was coming from somewhere far away, a place I couldn't reach. And her eyes—God, her eyes—they weren't hers. Not really. They lacked that fire, that intensity that had always been her defining trait. It felt like I had been talking to a ghost. A memory, not a person.

Then it hit me, like a punch straight to the chest—this wasn't Aadhira. At least, not the Aadhira I knew. My breath caught as the truth ripped through me. I hadn't been speaking to a breathing person. I had been face-to-face with her spirit. A remnant of the woman she once was, holding on for a reason I couldn't understand.

Aadhira was dead.

The words clawed at the back of my mind, refusing to settle. She had died in pursuit of this truth, but somehow, she had come back, driven by something stronger than death. A message. A warning. And now, it was mine to carry. The files in my hand seemed to throb with meaning, no longer just papers. They were soaked in the weight of blood and despair, left for me to make sense of. It was her fight. Her unfinished business. Now it was mine.

I had to find Dev. It was the last thing Aadhira had said before she faded, her spirit mentioning his name like it was tethered to something far deeper than friendship. And I wasn't about to ignore it. Not now.

Days blurred together as I searched relentlessly for him, sleepless and haunted by a sense of urgency I couldn't shake. Each lead felt colder than the last, each face a dead end. But finally, in a quiet cafe, tucked away from prying eyes, I found him.

The place seemed innocent enough—just the scent of coffee and low conversations floating in the air. But there was an undercurrent of something else, something unseen. I approached him slowly, feeling the weight of what I was about to say pressing down on my chest. Dev looked up at me, surprise flashing in his eyes, quickly followed by concern.

I sat down across from him, the surreal sense of dread hanging over me like a dark cloud. How could I even explain what I had seen? How could I make him believe in something that I was still struggling to grasp myself? But as I spoke, laying out the horror of it all, I saw something shift in Dev's expression. The disbelief crumbled away, replaced by a grim understanding. He knew, just as I did, that there was no turning back.

My voice wavered as I spoke. "There's something you need to see." The finality of my words left no room for doubt.

Together, we made our way to Aadhira's house. The air seemed heavier as we approached, like the place had taken on the weight of her absence. It wasn't a home anymore; it was a mausoleum. Silent. Still. As we walked through the hallway, the framed photos on the walls felt like they were watching us, memories frozen in time, tinged with sadness.

When we reached the door to her study, I hesitated. Then, with a deep breath, I pushed it open.

The room was a mess of scattered papers, maps pinned to the walls, and photos that told a story only she had pieced together. It was chaos, but there was a method to it. I could feel her presence lingering in the air, like she had been trying to tell us something, right until the end.

On the desk, her laptop still glowed faintly. An unsent email stared back at us, its subject line glaring: "URGENT: Evidence Enclosed." The attachments held the secrets she had uncovered, the very ones she had been killed for. And beside it, a small package—wrapped, addressed, ready to be sent. But it never had been. Fate had seen to that.

Dev took it all in, the weight of her work, the unfinished story she had left behind. Then the room shifted. A soft light filled the space, glowing brighter, casting long shadows across the floor. It was the same light I had seen in the forest—the orb of energy that had greeted Aadhira in her last moments.

"She's guiding us," I whispered, unable to tear my eyes away.

The light moved toward the door, beckoning us to follow. And we did. Without hesitation, Dev and I followed the ethereal glow, deeper into the night, into the forest. Every sound around us felt amplified—the rustling leaves, the snapping branches—all of it seemed alive, humming with energy. The light led us to a small clearing, the ground freshly disturbed.

It stopped above the earth, hovering, before slowly sinking into the soil. Dev dropped to his knees, his breath shallow as he dug. I joined him, my hands clawing at the earth, until wood showed beneath the surface.

The crate. It was ancient, weathered, but it held everything we had been chasing. Everything Aadhira had died for.

As Dev touched it, something changed. The forest disappeared, and he was gone—thrust into Aadhira's last moments. I could see it in his face, the way his body tensed, his eyes distant. He was living it, feeling her fear, her determination. I watched as tears welled in his eyes, the weight of her death settling on him.

When the vision ended, he was back, trembling but resolute. Together, we opened the crate. Inside were the remains—the bones of Aadhira and her allies, hidden away, forgotten. But there was more. A file, half-buried but preserved. It held the last pieces of the puzzle.

Dev's hands shook as he reached for it. This wasn't just evidence. It was her legacy. And now, it was our responsibility to see it through.

"We have to finish this," I said, my voice barely a whisper.

Dev nodded, the fire in his eyes matching the determination I had once seen in Aadhira. This wasn't just about justice anymore. It was about honoring her memory, telling her story, and making sure the truth finally came to light.

As we left the clearing, the first rays of dawn broke through the trees. The darkness was lifting, but our journey was far from over. Aadhira's voice echoed in my mind, her last words clear and unwavering.

"Tell our story."

And we would.

XI

The Veil of Shadows

We moved through the forest, each step deliberate, each breath shallow. The first light of dawn was creeping in, a pale glow barely touching the edges of the thick foliage that kept us shrouded in shadow. The orb—our strange, phantom guide—floated ahead, leading us once again to the clearing. This was where Aadhira and the others had met their brutal end. I could still smell the freshly disturbed earth where we unearthed the crate.

"Do you think she'll find peace now?" Dev's voice cut through the suffocating silence, barely loud enough to reach me.

I didn't answer right away. My eyes stayed on the patch of ground where we had uncovered the remains, as if it held the answers I didn't want to face. "I don't know," I finally said, my voice low. "But whatever comes next... this isn't over. It's just the beginning."

The orb flickered as if it heard me, pulsing with a strange intensity, its glow brightening just enough to catch my attention. It hovered between us, a silent command drawing our focus back to the forest.

"There's more," Dev whispered, though neither of us knew exactly what waited ahead.

Every instinct told me to turn back, to leave this cursed place, and never look back. But something deeper, something primal, held me here. Since the moment I realized what Aadhira had become, the pull was undeniable. I glanced at Dev, and in that brief look, I knew we were thinking the same thing. We weren't done here.

Without another word, we moved deeper into the forest, the clearing—and everything it held—fading behind us. But no matter how far we walked, I knew one thing: we couldn't leave the past behind. Not yet.

☙

The air shifted, heavier now, gripping tight around my chest. Every breath felt labored, as if the forest itself was closing in on us. The trees—those twisted, ancient sentinels—seemed alive with malice, their gnarled branches contorted into expressions of agony. With each step, the weight of the unseen pressed down harder, a suffocating presence that whispered of horrors untold.

"This place..." Dev's voice was barely a whisper. I could hear the dread curling in his words, rising from deep within, like something he couldn't swallow back down.

The orb flickered, its glow dimming, faltering like a candle caught in a gust of wind. I hadn't noticed it before, but now I saw it—this wasn't just a guide. It was struggling. Whatever force kept it alight was weakening the deeper into this cursed forest we went.

The orb led us off the path, into a thicket where the trees were older, their roots like skeletal hands clawing through the earth. There was barely any life here. The few plants that clung to the ground were grey, twisted, like they'd been poisoned by something unseen.

The orb dimmed further, settling over a patch of ground between two ancient trunks. A strange, ghostly mist rose from the earth, and I exchanged a glance with Dev. We didn't need to speak. We both knew there was something here.

I knelt, brushing the dead leaves aside with trembling fingers. The soil beneath was warm—too warm—like something was still alive under there, breathing. A shiver ran through me as I heard it—a deep sigh from the roots, a sorrowful whisper that seemed to seep out of the earth itself.

Then I saw it. A corner of metal, peeking out from under the dirt. My heart lurched as I reached for it, brushing away more soil. It was a tarnished handle, attached to something larger—a box, much like the crate we had found earlier.

"Another one?" Dev muttered, his voice thick with disbelief. "Just like the crate."

I nodded, my throat too tight to speak. We worked in silence, hands moving faster, adrenaline pushing through us through the dread. The chest was heavy, iron and rusted with age, but intact. Together, we pried it from the earth and forced the lid open. It groaned in protest, a sound that echoed unnaturally in the forest's silence.

A foul stench hit us immediately—rot mixed with something sulfuric, burning the back of my throat. But it wasn't bones we found inside. No, this was something worse.

The chest was filled with artefacts. Objects that didn't belong together, but somehow did. Old, worn documents with dates from the 1800s, a faded photograph of a family standing in front of a bungalow that nagged at my memory. There were toys, a rusted jewelry box, cracked spectacles—items belonging to people long forgotten, people whose lives had ended in tragedy.

"These..." Dev's voice trembled with the realization. "These are graves. That crate, this chest... They're all graves. Memorials for those who were erased."

I stared at the artefacts, each one carrying the weight of a life lost, a story untold. And suddenly, it clicked. The orb wasn't just guiding us. It was leading us to the souls who had been wronged, whose suffering still lingered here.

Dev rifled through the papers with a growing urgency, scanning for anything that made sense. But most of it was written in an old, unfamiliar dialect—parts of Malayalam, mixed with something else. He pulled out a ledger, its pages yellowed and crumbling. Rows of names, dates beside them, etched in faded ink.

One name jumped out at me: Anand Varma. I had seen it before, somewhere buried in an obscure record.

But the name beneath it stopped my breath cold: Devika Varma.

I held the ledger up to Dev, my hands shaking. He stared at it, his face paling as he traced the name with trembling fingers.

"She... she was my ancestor," he whispered, his voice breaking. "My great-great-grandmother. My family never spoke of her much. All I knew was that she disappeared."

We stood in stunned silence, the weight of this discovery crushing down on us. This wasn't just our burden anymore. It spanned generations—something dark, twisted, and ancient, pulling its threads through time.

I turned back to the orb, now a faint glow beside the chest. "What do we do now?" I asked, but I already knew the answer. The task was ours.

The ground trembled beneath us, a soft rumbling that echoed through the trees. A storm was coming—both in the air and on the ground. The orb suddenly flared brightly, casting long shadows that danced wildly against the trees. It zipped forward, guiding us once more, back toward the clearing where Aadhira's remains had been uncovered.

We didn't hesitate. We followed, shutting the chest behind us, leaving its dark secrets buried once more. The wind picked up, tearing through the trees as we moved faster. Thunder rumbled in the distance, a warning that the storm was closing in.

When we reached the clearing, the wind was howling, shaking the trees to their roots. The earth trembled beneath our feet, a living force. The orb's light was faint now, barely enough to hold back the encroaching darkness.

And then we saw it. A figure emerging from the shadows.

It wasn't Aadhira. This was something older, something far more dangerous. It moved with a slow, deliberate grace, dragging the darkness with it like a suffocating cloak. When it breathed in, the entire forest seemed to hold its breath.

We stood our ground, hearts pounding, as the figure stopped at the edge of the clearing. It wore tattered robes, regal once, now decayed. Its face—an emaciated mask—was frozen in eternal suffering, its hollow eyes boring into us.

The wind howled as the figure spoke, its voice a broken whisper, drenched in torment. "You... seek to awaken the dead..."

My throat was dry, but I spoke. "Who... who are you?"

The figure tilted its head, a grotesque mimicry of thought. "I was once Devika Varma... I was once alive... Now I am a memory... a curse..."

I glanced at Dev, his face as pale as the spectre before us. His ancestor—lost to time, bound to this land by a curse neither of us could fully comprehend.

"What happened to you?" Dev's voice cracked, barely above a whisper.

The spectre shifted, its form flickering as if it might dissolve into the wind. "I was betrayed... like Aadhira... I was buried here... cursed to this unholy ground."

Her words hung heavy in the air, thick with the pain of generations. If we were going to end this, we needed answers.

"Tell us," I urged. "Help us understand, so we can end it."

Devika's spectre wavered, and the surrounding forest seemed to warp, bending time and space. The trees faded, replaced by the grand outlines of a forgotten estate, flickering like a memory. The Varma Estate—its walls, once majestic, now burned with the anger and betrayal that had destroyed it.

"They killed me because I found something..." Devika's voice was a whisper carried by the wind. "An ancient pact... I tried to protect our bloodline... Instead, I cursed it."

We watched as the past unfolded around us—whispers of power and betrayal, deals made in the shadows, the lives taken to preserve the Varma legacy. And in that moment, everything became clear. Aadhira's death, Devika's fate, the murders—connected by a curse that had bound the land and its people for generations.

The vision faded, and we were left standing in the clearing once more. Devika's spectre was gone, but her presence lingered, along with the countless souls still trapped here, their whispers carried on the wind.

"Now we know," I said, my voice hoarse. "Now we know what they did."

"But how do we end it?" Dev's voice was low, haunted.

The orb flickered in response, dim but steady, showing us the way forward.

And as the storm bore down on us, Dev and I followed it. We knew this was the end—whatever waited ahead; we had to face it.

The forest was no longer just a forest. It was a battleground between the living and the dead.

XII

Inheritance of Shadows

The forest whispered our names as we pushed deeper into its dark, suffocating heart. The orb of light floated ahead, pulsing with energy that felt more alive than anything around us, casting eerie shadows that twisted and stretched like ghosts. Each step felt heavier, the air thick, pressing down on me, like the very trees were watching, waiting for us to stumble.

I glanced over at Dev. His face was tight, a mask of fear and determination, like he was wrestling with everything we'd uncovered. His eyes flicked between the orb and the forest, never settling on one thing for too long. He knew, as well as I did, that we weren't alone. Whatever waited for us wasn't here to welcome us.

"What do you think we'll find?" My voice barely broke the silence, almost swallowed by the oppressive night. Even then, I couldn't hide the tremor that slipped through.

Dev didn't answer right away. His silence was heavy, and when he finally spoke, his voice was hoarse. "Answers. Or maybe... maybe just an end."

The orb dimmed slightly, like it was fighting to stay lit, as we moved forward. The forest thickened around us, the trees older, their gnarled branches twisted into grotesque shapes. A narrow trail appeared before us, barely visible, like a path forgotten by time.

Dev stopped, his eyes locked on the trail ahead. "This is it. We're close."

I followed his gaze. "What is it?"

"Sarpakavu," Dev whispered. His voice was distant, like he was speaking more to the forest than to me. "A serpent grove. The old places... where spirits guard what shouldn't be disturbed."

I knew enough of the stories to understand the weight of his words. Serpent groves, sacred and forbidden, were places where men weren't meant to tread. The air felt heavier now, as though even speaking the name brought the curse closer. Still, the orb moved ahead, pulling us forward.

We followed, memories of old stories clawing at the back of my mind. The deeper we went, the more the air thickened, every breath a struggle. The smell of rotting leaves and damp soil clung to everything, as though the forest was alive with decay. Time felt strange here, slow and suffocating, like we were moving through something much older than ourselves.

At last, the trail opened into a clearing. The orb flared one final time, then dimmed, just enough to reveal the scene before us.

Dev froze.

An altar stood in the center, ancient and slick with moss, its stones worn from centuries of offerings. Draped over it was a cloth, its gold threads faded but still glinting faintly in the dim light. Behind the altar, an enormous tree rose, its roots twisted around the stones like they were holding something down, keeping it trapped.

The bark shimmered like scales, and I felt a frigid chill run down my spine. A trail of offerings led to the altar—wilted flowers, burnt-out lamps, food long gone to rot. Everything about this place felt wrong, soaked in something ancient, something hungry.

I stepped closer, drawn to the carvings etched into the altar. Serpents. Their eyes seemed to follow me, watching, waiting. "This... this is older than the Varma family. Their power... it came from here?"

Dev didn't answer. His hand reached out, almost like he wasn't in control, fingers brushing the stone serpents. The moment he touched them, the forest seemed to stop, holding its breath.

A voice filled the air, soft and cold, coming from everywhere and nowhere all at once.

"Come closer, Dev... lay down the burden. Be free from what has been done..."

I grabbed Dev's shoulder, grounding him as panic crept up my spine. "What was that?"

Dev didn't answer. His eyes were locked on the altar, the orb flickering wildly now, as though it were fighting something. Then I saw it—a depression in the center of the altar, surrounded by serpent eyes, like the focus of some ancient ritual.

Dev reached into his bag and pulled out the stone we had found earlier, the one from the chest, covered in strange inscriptions. My gut twisted. I wasn't sure what it was for, but I knew this was part of something much bigger, something older than either of us could understand.

He placed the stone in the depression, and the orb exploded into light, so bright it forced me to shield my eyes. When I looked again, the stone had sunk into place with a click, like a key turning in a lock.

The tree shuddered, its branches trembling, sending a rain of leaves down around us. The carvings on the altar glowed, pulsing with fiery light, tracing the serpents in bright, living lines.

The orb flickered one last time, then vanished, leaving us in near-darkness. The carvings were the only light now, dim and ominous.

The ground shook beneath us, and I stumbled back, my heart pounding in my throat. "What the hell is happening?!"

Before Dev could answer, the earth split open beneath the altar, and with a deep, guttural hiss, something rose. The roots of the tree parted, and from the ground, a massive scaled form emerged.

A serpent.

Its body was enormous, its scales shimmering in the faint light, and its eyes burned with a rage that felt centuries old. It rose higher, coiling around the tree, its gaze fixed on Dev, and I felt its anger—a deep, simmering fury that had been waiting for this moment.

"You cannot escape what is owed..." the voice hissed again, this time coming from the serpent itself.

I stumbled back, terror gripping me. "Dev, we have to get out of here!"

But Dev stood his ground, eyes locked on the serpent. He knew, just as I did, that there was no running. This was tied to his blood, his family. He was the key. He had to end this.

Steeling himself, Dev stepped forward, toward the altar, toward the massive serpent. "I'm here," he whispered, more to himself than to the creature. "I'm here to end this."

The serpent loomed above him, its body coiled, eyes burning with an ancient fire. It didn't strike, but its presence weighed heavily on us both, pressing down like a vice.

I could feel the power in the air crackling around us, pulling at something deep inside Dev. He reached into the bag, pulling out more of the stones we had found, three more, each one glowing faintly. He handed them to me, his voice steady despite the fear in his eyes.

"We need to place these in the altar. All of them."

I nodded, my hands shaking as I took the stones. Together, we placed each one on the altar, and with each stone, the carvings grew brighter, the ground beneath us shaking more violently.

With the last stone set, the altar shattered, the ground opening beneath it. The serpent let out a roar, its body thrashing, sending debris flying. The air crackled with energy, and I was thrown to the ground, the world spinning around me.

When I looked up, the serpent towered above us, its massive body coiled around the tree, its eyes fixed on Dev. And then, as if seeing something deep inside him, it stopped.

"You are bound by blood," the serpent hissed, its voice softer now, almost a whisper. "What was taken must be returned."

Dev stepped forward, his face pale, but his voice steady. "I'm here to end this."

The serpent lowered its head, and for a moment, the world stood still. Dev raised his hand, and in the faint light, I saw the blade he had pulled from his bag—a small, ancient knife, its edge worn but sharp.

He looked at me, his eyes filled with something I couldn't name. "This is the only way."

Before I could stop him, before I could say anything, Dev raised the blade to his palm and drew it across his skin, blood welling up and dripping onto the altar.

The serpent reared back, its body writhing, and with a final, deafening roar, it collapsed into the earth, its massive form crumbling into dust.

The ground stilled, the air grew quiet, and for the first time since we entered the forest, I felt the weight of it all lift.

Dev collapsed to his knees, his breath ragged, the knife falling from his hand.

I rushed to him, grabbing his shoulders, shaking him. "Dev! Dev, are you okay?"

He nodded weakly, his eyes glazed but alive. "It's over," he whispered, his voice barely audible. "It's finally over."

We sat there in the forest's silence, the weight of everything that had happened pressing down on us. But for the first time in what felt like forever, I believed him.

It was over.

XIII

Ancestral Lament

Dev gasped as consciousness clawed its way back to him, like a net being pulled from deep water. His breath was ragged, his body heavy, sinking into the damp earth as if the ground itself sought to drag him down. He blinked against the darkness, the faint echoes of the serpent's wail still ringing in his ears.

I watched as he stirred, the stillness around us thick and unnatural. His arm was covered in blood, a jagged stone embedded in his flesh. He grimaced, pushing himself into a sitting position, pain etched across his face as the broken landscape revealed itself. The once-sacred Sarpakavu lay in ruins—uprooted trees, shattered earth, and the altar that had once stood tall was now nothing more than debris scattered beneath the lifeless trunk of the ancient tree.

I could see the fear in Dev's eyes. He was asking the same question as I was—What had the serpent's irrevocable act unleashed?

A sudden rustle broke the silence, and he turned sharply toward me. I was slumped against a broken log, my head throbbing, blood caked on my forehead. I could feel his relief when our eyes met, but it was short-lived. We were still in danger.

"Ramesh!" Dev's voice was hoarse, cracking through the tension that hung in the air. He crawled over to me, wincing with every movement as his injured arm trailed blood across the earth.

I forced myself to stir, blinking through the dizziness. My chest heaved as I tried to catch my breath, the air thick with the stench of death and decay. He reached me, and I felt his hand on my shoulder, steadying me, grounding me in the chaos that surrounded us. Together, we pulled ourselves to our feet, the weight of our survival bearing down on us.

The clearing was wrecked, nothing but devastation. Dev scanned the ruins, his eyes narrowing as if searching for any trace of the ritual. But there was nothing. The serpent was gone, the altar destroyed, and the air hummed with an energy that made my skin crawl. Whatever we had done, it hadn't lifted the curse—it had made it worse. The darkness wasn't gone. It had only been awakened.

We stumbled through the forest, the path we had once taken now choked with roots and broken branches. Each step was a fight against the groaning earth beneath us, the forest lamenting its destruction. A stiff wind whipped through the trees, bringing with it the unmistakable scent of rot and something far older. The fog was rising, coiling around our legs as if the forest itself was trying to hold us back.

It felt like hours before we finally broke free of the cursed grove. The air beyond the trees was thin, lighter, though the weight of the forest still clung to us. As we approached the village, the small huts and distant hearths seemed serene in the moonlight. But I knew better than to trust it.

Dev's pace slowed as a new sound reached our ears—a low, keening wail that echoed through the quiet night. It was the sound of grief, raw and ancient, rising from the earth itself. As we drew closer, the source became apparent. Women were gathered outside the small temple, their voices raised in lamentation, hands pressed to their faces in mourning.

"There's no smoke," Dev muttered beside me, his eyes scanning the village, taking in the darkened chimneys, the absence of life.

"Where is everyone?" I asked, but my voice trailed off as I noticed something strange. No one was reacting to us. The villagers didn't turn or acknowledge our presence as we approached. It was as if we were invisible outsiders not meant to be part of their grief.

A chill settled in my gut, deepening the sense of unease. Something was wrong. I could feel it in the way the villagers moved, in the hollow sound of their cries.

Then, we saw her—Narayani Amma, the village oracle. She sat alone at the entrance to the temple, her body trembling, her eyes glazed with knowledge she didn't want to hold. She was the only one who noticed us.

Her lips quivered as her body convulsed, the unmistakable signs of a trance taking hold. I instinctively stepped back, wary of what was coming.

"The serpent…" she whispered, her voice cracked and dry. "It heralds a death that cannot be undone. The bones of the land will remember."

Dev froze, his face pale. I saw him glance at her, his arm still bleeding, his eyes wide with fear. Her words wrapped around him like chains, tightening with each breath.

Before I could react, Narayani Amma lurched forward, gripping Dev's arm with a strength that seemed impossible for her frail body. Her fingers dug into his flesh, into the blood still flowing from his wound.

"You're one of them now," she rasped, her eyes wild and hollow. "The curse has found a new vessel."

I watched as Dev's expression shifted from confusion to terror. He tried to pull away, but her grip was iron. "I don't understand," he muttered, his voice trembling, his mind racing back to the ritual, the serpent, the altar. Everything was coming apart, and now this—the curse was still alive, and it had found him.

Narayani Amma's eyes bore into him. "This land—it isn't done with you. The serpent eats its tail. You must go back. Find the origin."

With a last gasp, she released him, collapsing to the ground in a convulsion. The other villagers didn't even react, still lost in their grief. The sight of it all—the wailing, the ignored collapse, the cryptic words—was enough to send cold sweat trickling down my spine. This wasn't over.

I grabbed Dev, yanking him back. "We need to go. Now."

His breath came in short, frantic bursts as he stumbled away from the square. I could feel his fear, the weight of Narayani Amma's words pressing down on him like a physical force. We had heard of things like this before—stories whispered in the dark, of madness that crept into men's souls, driving them to disappear, to lose themselves in the very forest we had just escaped.

We fled the village, the cries of the women fading behind us, but still echoing in our minds. Neither of us spoke much as we trudged through the darkness, our exhaustion palpable. Dev's arm bled steadily, each step a reminder of the curse still lingering over us.

By the time we reached the edge of the forest, the sky was brightening, the first light of dawn chasing away the shadows. We found an abandoned bungalow near the old plantation, its walls cracked and crumbling, but it gave us some small sense of safety.

We needed rest. Both of us were beyond exhaustion, our bodies and minds pushed to the limit. But as we lay there, the whispers of the past swirled in the wind outside. The land wasn't done with us yet. I could feel it in the air, in the way the forest seemed to sigh as the morning light touched its edges.

Whatever we had unleashed in the serpent grove, it was still with us, and I knew deep down—it was only the beginning.

ॐ

The sunlight barely warmed the room when Dev stirred again. Its faint glow filtered through the cracked walls and broken windows, casting long, weak shadows. I watched as he tore what remained of his sleeves, using the fabric to fashion a rough bandage for his wound. He winced as he tightened it, the pain clear on his face, but he didn't say a word.

I sat by the window, staring out into the distance, my mind still trapped in the darkness we'd left behind. The events from the night before churned in my thoughts, their weight dragging at my very soul. I could feel the curse lingering, like a presence that refused to leave, even in the daylight. I didn't want to ask, but the question burned inside me until I finally spoke. "The curse—what does it want? Does it ever end?"

Dev didn't answer right away. I could tell he didn't know. The silence between us felt like a judgment, like the land itself had its own plans, and we were just pawns in a game too old for us to understand. I could feel it—whatever had taken root here was much bigger than us, older than the village, deeper than anything we could see.

He didn't look at me when he spoke. "I don't think it ends, Ramesh. Not like we hoped."

That truth gnawed at me. My stomach twisted, not just from fear, but from the dawning realization that the curse wasn't something we could simply escape. It was a cycle—an ancient, unbroken chain that would keep feeding on whatever was tied to the land, until it had claimed enough.

I reached into my jacket, my hand brushing against something I hadn't even remembered carrying with me. A small pendant—an amulet that my mother had given me long ago. I had thought little of it was just an old family trinket. But now, in the frosty morning light, the symbol carved into its surface seemed eerily familiar. It matched the carvings we'd seen at the ritual site. I pulled it out, holding it between us.

Dev noticed immediately, his eyes narrowing as he studied it. "What is that?"

I hesitated, feeling a weight in my chest. "My mother's," I whispered, my voice barely holding steady. "She used to say it protects against the Serpent's gaze. I never believed her. Thought it was just superstition." I paused, looking at the pendant, then at him. "But now..."

"Now we need all the protection we can get," he finished for me. His mind seemed to work faster, already moving past the object in my hand and into something deeper. I could see it in his eyes—he was connecting the dots, trying to piece together what the curse really was.

He didn't say it out loud, but I could sense his thoughts. What if the serpent wasn't just some ghost haunting his family? What if it had been feeding off the Varma lineage for generations, waiting for the right moment to fully reassert itself? Dev's connection to this curse wasn't just about his ancestors anymore—it was alive now, in him.

We needed answers. Proper answers. If Narayani Amma was right and Dev had become the new vessel, we had to understand what that meant. If we didn't, it wouldn't just consume him—it would take us both. There were places we hadn't explored yet, parts of the forest that hid deeper secrets. I knew there had to be something else out there, something that could explain what we were up against.

Dev reached out and took the pendant from my hand. His bruised fingers closed around it, and I saw the tension in his jaw as he studied the symbol. He said nothing, but the look in his eyes told me everything. He felt it too—the feeling that something was watching us, lurking just beyond our vision, waiting for us to make the next move. Whatever it was, it would not leave us alone. Not now.

The air in the room felt heavy, thick with something unseen but tangible. It wrapped around us, pulling at my thoughts, whispering to me in a way that I couldn't shake. Narayani Amma had told us to seek the origin, to go deeper. But what if going deeper only made it worse? What if unraveling the curse set something even darker into motion?

I wasn't sure I wanted to know. But we had no choice. The edge between life and death, between curse and freedom, was slipping away, and I could feel the pull leading us back into the darkness. There was no turning back now.

Dev's grip tightened on the pendant, his knuckles turning white as he set his jaw. I could see the resolve hardening in him, the same feeling rising in me. We didn't have all the answers, but we knew enough to understand that whatever was waiting for us, we had to face it.

"We need to go back," Dev said, his voice quiet but firm. "Deeper than before. We need to find the source."

I nodded. The forest hadn't let us go, and neither had the curse. We were bound to this now, as much a part of it as the land itself. We gathered what little strength we had left, knowing that the next steps would take us further into the heart of the curse than we had ever imagined.

The sunlight might have broken through the clouds, but the shadows were still with us. And they weren't done yet.

XIV

The Darkness Within

Dawn came grudgingly, the sky still thick with dark clouds, as if the light itself was too weary to push through. The mist clung to the village like a shroud, muting everything in sight. The weight of the night before—those terrible moments of grief and despair—hung in the air, refusing to fade with the morning.

Dev sat by the window, his gaze distant, fixed on the deserted village square. I could see the tension in his posture, the way his breath fogged the glass in small bursts. I sat on the floor, absently turning the small amulet over in my hand. It had been my family's, but now it felt like a lifeline, a thin barrier between us and the curse that had woven itself into everything.

Neither of us spoke. The silence between us was thick, filled with questions neither of us dared to ask. Dev hadn't been the same since Narayani Amma's words had marked him as the vessel. He knew it too—the way his eyes clouded, the way he seemed to wrestle with something inside himself. This curse was in his blood, and now it was clawing its way to the surface.

I couldn't hold back any longer. "We've got to move fast, Dev. Staying here... I don't know what might happen."

He didn't answer right away. His face twisted, like he was trying to suppress something, something dark and growing stronger by the moment. I watched as he clenched his fists, his knuckles white. The curse—it wasn't just a lingering shadow anymore. It was becoming part of him.

Dev, with a strained but firm voice, finally said, "We leave at first light. Find where this started and end it."

I nodded, though the doubt in my mind remained. "And if it can't be ended?"

Dev's eyes darkened as he looked out into the distance. "Then so be it. If I'm the vessel, I won't go down without a fight."

The forest had changed. As we pushed deeper, the familiar trails and landmarks had twisted into something darker, more menacing. The trees loomed overhead, their gnarled branches reaching out like claws. The ground beneath us was slick with mud and rot, the air thick with the smell of decay. It felt like the forest itself had turned against us.

The amulet, which I had tied around Dev's neck for protection, grew colder with every step. The deeper we went, the more certain I became we were heading toward something ancient, something powerful. Dev spoke little, but I could see it in his eyes—the same unease, the same sense of inevitability. We were walking straight into the curse's heart.

The silence between us grew, but it wasn't an empty silence. It was as though the forest was listening, waiting.

The curse was alive, and it knew we were coming.

After hours of trudging through the dense forest, we stumbled into a clearing. In the center stood a massive tree, its bark scarred with deep carvings that spiraled upward. Tattered clothes hung from the branches, swaying slightly in the breeze—offerings from those who had come before us. The air felt heavier here, like the very ground was watching us.

"This is the place," I whispered, my breath catching in my throat. "It has to be."

Dev didn't answer. He stepped forward, drawn to the tree like it was calling to him. The amulet around his neck grew colder, and I saw him wince as he touched the carvings. The symbols told stories—of betrayal, of bloodshed, of curses invoked in dark rituals.

"This is where it started," I whispered, feeling the weight of the history pressing down on us. "The first Varma betrayed his people here. The land remembers. It cursed your entire bloodline."

Dev's face paled as he stared at the carvings. His hand trembled against the bark, and before I could react, blood trickled down his arm. But it wasn't his blood—it was the tree's. His hands pressed into the carvings, and the tree responded, bleeding through him. The earth trembled beneath us, and I saw panic flash in his eyes.

"Dev, you're bleeding!" I shouted, rushing toward him. But he was already staggering backward, the blood still flowing from the tree's wounds, etching new symbols into the bark.

The ground shook harder. "We have to leave!" I yelled, but Dev didn't move. His eyes were closed, his face twisted in concentration as if he was trying to push something out of his mind. His hands clenched the air, and I could see the strain, the effort it took to resist whatever was invading his thoughts.

Then I saw it—the red eyes. They were there, not in the physical world, but in Dev's mind, staring back at him with an ancient power that pulsed through the air.

Why do you seek the end? The voice reverberated through the ground, through the trees, through Dev.

He opened his eyes, but the clearing had vanished. He was standing in a shadowy version of the same forest, colder, darker, with shadows that moved on their own. Before him stood a woman, her figure draped in tattered robes, her skin pale and cracked like an old stone. Her eyes—those same red eyes—burned from beneath wild, matted hair.

"Who are you?" Dev demanded, his voice low, each word dragging through the weight of her presence.

The woman's lips parted, but no words came out. Instead, she growled, a low, monstrous sound that sent chills through the air. "I am the curse," she hissed. "You are my tether. You are the vessel."

Dev's body tensed, his hands shaking as her presence pressed against him, crushing him with the weight of a thousand years of rage and sorrow. But something inside him pushed back. He would not let her take him.

"I won't be your pawn," he spat through gritted teeth.

Her red eyes flared, and the air grew stiflingly hot. His skin felt like it was peeling away, the heat unbearable. She grinned, a twisted smile filled with malice. "If you won't play your role, then others will bleed for it."

The vision shattered, and Dev collapsed to the ground, gasping for air. I rushed to him, convulsing him, trying to pull him back.

"Dev! Dev, wake up!" My voice cracked with fear as the tremors beneath us grew stronger. The earth was splitting, and the tree groaned like it was about to collapse in on itself.

Dev looked up at me, his face pale, his eyes wide with terror. "Go!" he rasped, shoving me away. "Go now!"

"I'm not leaving you!" I shouted back, my heart pounding in my chest. The ground split open, and the roots of the tree rose, pulling at the earth, threatening to drag us under.

A wave of energy exploded from the tree, knocking us both off our feet. I hit the ground hard; the impact forcing the air from my lungs. But even through the haze of pain, I could see the woman's figure, standing in the center of the clearing, her red eyes burning with ancient fury.

"What do we do, Dev?" I screamed, scrambling to my feet. "What do we do?"

Dev gritted his teeth, fighting to control the curse surging within him. He grabbed the amulet from around his neck and, with a fierce determination, hurled it toward the tree. His voice rose in a chant, ancient words pouring from his lips, words he didn't know but that had been seared into his mind by the vision.

The amulet burst into light, a dazzling flare that filled the clearing, engulfing the tree and the woman in a radiant blaze. The red-eyed figure let out a screech, a sound so horrifying it cut straight to my bones. But the light grew brighter, surrounding her and the tree until everything was consumed.

Then, silence.

Dev collapsed beside me, his body limp. The curse's hold on him weakened, but not gone. Darkness closed in around us both, and I felt the earth give way beneath us.

When I awoke, we were deep underground, in a cavern lit by soft, glowing ferns. The walls shimmered with moisture, and the air was cold and damp. I pushed myself up, aching all over. Dev lay next to me, unconscious but breathing.

I didn't know where we were, but I knew one thing—the curse wasn't done with us. We had fought back, but it still held us in its grip, waiting, watching. We were in its domain now, and it would not let us go easily.

XV
Whispers of Time

The earth rumbled beneath us, a deep, unsettling tremor that seemed to resonate with Dev's thoughts. He hesitated behind me, his steps slowing as if the weight of the cavern pressed down on him harder with every breath. The air was thick, musty with the scent of decay and something ancient, something that should have stayed buried. It felt like we weren't supposed to be here, like the land itself was pushing back against our presence.

The darkness wasn't just around us—it was in the air, in our minds, seeping into every crack of our courage. My flashlight barely cut through it, the beam flickering as if it, too, was struggling to hold on. The walls were slick, wet with moisture that pulsed like the stone had its own heartbeat.

Dev stayed a few steps behind, silent but close. I knew he felt it, too—the wrongness of this place. Every step forward felt like a violation, like we were trespassing somewhere that had never known light.

"We've been through too much, Dev," I muttered, not looking back. "Friends don't abandon each other, even if it means walking through hell."

He didn't respond at first. When he finally spoke, his voice was strained, his words heavy. "I don't want to drag you down with me."

"Too late for that," I said, the bitter laugh escaping me before I could stop it.

The tunnel opened into a vast chamber, the scent of wet earth almost suffocating. Our lights swept across the space, revealing towering columns covered in ancient symbols—grotesque carvings of twisted figures writhing in agony. I didn't need to say it. This was a place of sacrifice, a shrine to something dark and unspeakable.

"These carvings..." I trailed my hand across the rough surface, the symbols sharp and unsettling under my fingers. "They're older than anything we've seen. This place—it wasn't built for anything good."

Dev stepped closer, his face tight as he studied the symbols. They were brutal, depicting suffering and torment, curved lines twisting into grotesque shapes. His eyes darkened as he stared at the carvings, the fear in him growing with every second.

"This isn't just a shrine," he said, his voice low. "It's a place of sacrifice."

The words hung in the air, a weight pressing down on us. I felt the cold dread creeping along my spine as we moved deeper into the chamber. The carvings became more vivid, the tortured faces leaping out from the stone, their eyes wide with terror, their mouths twisted in silent screams.

Then I saw it—a section of the wall that stopped me in my tracks. "Dev," I said, my voice barely above a whisper. "Look at this."

He moved beside me, his gaze locking on the mural. It showed a figure in royal garb, standing over a river of blood, watching as those around him writhed in pain. The figure's face was unmistakable—it was one of his ancestors. His family's bloodline had been at the center of this horror for centuries.

Dev's breath caught in his throat. "Varma…this was one of my ancestors." His voice cracked, the weight of the truth hitting him like a physical blow.

I didn't know what to say. The carvings, the sacrifices, the curse—it had all come from his bloodline. The weight of it hung between us like a suffocating presence. This wasn't just a curse—it was retribution for the sins of his family, an ancient wrong that demanded a price.

The surrounding air grew colder, thick with the stench of decay. I could hear Dev's breath quicken, the fear creeping into his voice as the light from our flashlights dimmed, swallowed by the shadows pressing in on us. The oppressive silence was shattered by a faint murmuring, a low chant that seemed to rise from the very walls.

"Do you hear that?" I whispered, my pulse racing.

Dev nodded, his eyes scanning the dark corners of the chamber. The chanting grew louder, filling the space with an ancient malice, a song of the dead who had never been granted peace.

A rustling sound came from the far end of the chamber. Our flashlights snapped toward the sound, revealing a figure—a decayed, leathery form that had once been a man, now a hollow shell. Its eyes glowed with a faint, red light, its mouth hanging open in a silent scream.

For a moment, neither of us moved. The figure glided toward us, its skeletal hands outstretched, a mournful wail rising from its hollow chest.

"Run!" Dev's shout broke the spell, and he shoved me forward. My legs moved on instinct, fear propelling me through the chamber as the creature's groaning filled the space behind us.

We ran, the ground beneath us trembling, the walls closing in like a living thing. The chanting grew louder, a deafening chorus that made my heart pound in my ears. Every step felt like we were sinking deeper into something dark and malevolent, something that wanted to consume us whole.

We burst into another chamber, smaller but no less suffocating. An altar sat in the center, its surface covered in dried blood, runes carved into the stone. The chanting reached a fever pitch, the very air vibrating with it.

"Where do we go?" I gasped, panic clawing at my chest as the skeletal remains hanging from the walls seemed to stare at us with empty eyes.

"We can't stay here!" Dev shouted, his voice barely audible over the thunderous chanting. The creature was closing in, its groaning filling the chamber like a death knell.

"The amulet!" I yelled, fumbling for the small pendant around my neck. "Maybe it can—"

But before I could finish, the room was plunged into darkness. The flashlights died, the chanting cut off, and a suffocating silence fell over us. I could feel the weight of something pressing against me, something cold and ancient.

Then, a whisper—close, right against my ear. "Traitors...all of you. You cannot escape."

My body jerked forward, an unseen force slamming me against the stone altar. I couldn't move, couldn't breathe, as something coiled around me, squeezing the life out of me. I could see Dev rushing toward me, his face twisted with fear, but he was too far, too late.

The creature hovered over me, its red eyes glowing, its skeletal hands sinking into my chest. The pain was indescribable, a fire burning through my veins, pulling at something deep inside me. I screamed, but no sound came out.

I was fading.

Then, through the haze of pain, I saw Dev's face, his eyes wide with determination. He held the amulet high, and in that moment, it blazed with a light so bright it filled the entire chamber. The creature screeched, a sound that tore through the air, and I felt the surrounding grip loosen.

Dev slammed the amulet onto my chest, and the creature dissolved in a flash of light, its scream echoing into nothingness. The walls of the chamber shook violently, slabs of stone crashing down around us.

I collapsed to the ground, gasping for air, my body trembling. Dev was beside me, his hands shaking as he lifted my head.

"You're okay," he whispered, his voice choked with relief. "I'm here. You're okay."

But I wasn't. My body felt like it had been drained of everything. My vision blurred, and I could barely feel the ground beneath me. I knew we had to move, but my limbs wouldn't respond.

Dev pulled me to my feet, half-dragging me out of the chamber, his voice urging me to keep going. We stumbled through the dark corridors; the walls pressing in on us as the curse pulsed through the air, alive and hungry.

We weren't free. Not yet.

The curse wasn't done with us. It was still there, waiting in the shadows, watching. And I knew, as we finally stepped into the chilly night air, that it would follow us wherever we went.

We had escaped, but we hadn't survived. Not really.

XVI
Voices of the Ghats

The darkness clung to the walls like the weight of a thousand cursed souls. Every step Dev took seemed to echo with lifetimes long gone—ancestors who had traded their very souls for power, bound by the same amulet that now trembled in his hand. The torchlight flickered, casting shadows that twisted around us like mocking spirits.

I leaned against the cold stone, my body heavy with the remnants of that harrowing possession. The weight wasn't just physical—I felt hollow, like something had been ripped out of me that couldn't be returned. Dev glanced at me, the worry in his eyes unmistakable. But what could he say? How could he even explain what had happened when I barely understood it myself?

"Ramesh," he whispered, his voice barely cutting through the thick silence. "We need to keep moving."

I nodded, but it felt like I was moving through a dream—or a nightmare. The carvings on the walls, the possession, the way the amulet flared with a life of its own... It was all too much. I pushed myself upright, feeling the cold seep into my bones. "What... what happened back there?" My voice cracked, barely above a whisper.

Dev hesitated. I could see the strain in his face, the weight of something he wasn't saying. "It tried to take you," he finally said, his voice tight. "The amulet—it fought it off. But I don't know how long it'll hold."

I swallowed hard; the words sinking in. I could feel it—the lingering presence of whatever had tried to claim me. The carvings on the walls, the twisted figures—they weren't just records. They were warnings. Whatever dark force had lured us here had been waiting. It had been watching for centuries.

"This place..." I muttered, looking around at the dark walls that seemed to pulse with malevolence. "It's been waiting for us, hasn't it? For you."

Dev didn't answer immediately, but his silence said more than words. This curse, this place—it had always been about him, about the bloodline that ran through his veins. The Varma family had built their legacy on something twisted, something dark. And now, we were both paying the price.

"We can't stop," Dev said, his voice sharp, pushing down the fear. "We need to keep going before it finds another way to break us."

I forced myself to keep moving, even though every instinct screamed for me to turn back. The air grew thicker as we pushed forward; the tunnel tightening around us like a throat closing in. Every step felt like we were being swallowed by the earth itself, as though the cavern was alive and trying to suffocate us.

The carvings on the walls grew more elaborate the deeper we went, the twisted figures becoming more grotesque, more lifelike. Each one seemed to scream silently, their faces frozen in eternal agony. The air shifted, growing colder, denser. I could feel it pressing down on my chest, each breath a struggle. I stopped, my breath catching in my throat.

"Do you feel that?" I rasped, my voice barely above a whisper.

Dev's eyes narrowed as he glanced around. He felt it too—the heavy, oppressive force closing in around us. The torchlight flickered, as if the very air was draining the light from it. The darkness pressed in, a living thing that pulsed in time with the beat of my heart.

"It's the tunnel," Dev muttered, his voice tight. But I could see in his eyes that he didn't believe it.

We pressed on, our pace quickening as the walls seemed to close in around us. I could feel something watching us, something ancient and malevolent. The shadows twisted, taking on shapes that whispered of long-buried horrors. Every step echoed in the silence, every breath seemed to stir the darkness.

We reached a vast chamber, and the air grew colder still. The ceiling rose high above us, lost in darkness. The walls were lined with carvings more intricate and terrifying than any we had seen. At the center of the chamber stood a massive stone altar, covered in symbols I couldn't understand, but their meaning was clear—sacrifice. Bones littered the surrounding ground, relics of forgotten rituals.

Dev's breath hitched as he looked at the altar, his eyes narrowing in recognition. He stepped forward; the torchlight flickering over the stone slab. "Do you think... this is it?"

Before I could answer, my eyes caught something—a staircase. Subtle, almost hidden, but unmistakable. It spiraled down, deeper into the earth.

"Look," I said, pointing. "There's more below."

Dev's pulse quickened, and I could see the conflict in his face. The descent felt inevitable, like a pull we couldn't resist. He clenched the amulet tighter, its warmth pulsing against his skin, as if it was both warning and guiding him.

"The answer's down there," he whispered. "I can feel it."

We exchanged a glance, both knowing that whatever waited at the bottom of those stairs was the heart of this curse, the irrevocable step in a journey we hadn't meant to take. And yet, we had no choice.

We descended.

The air grew colder as we spiraled downward, the walls closing in tighter with every step. The torch flickered, the flame barely clinging to life. I could feel it—the malevolent presence growing stronger the deeper we went, a pressure that made it hard to breathe.

Finally, we reached the bottom.

A smaller chamber, but somehow more oppressive than the one above. Black stone lined the walls, reflecting the faint light from our torch. In the center of the room was a pit, yawning open like the mouth of some ancient beast. Mist swirled inside, obscuring whatever lay within.

And then I saw him.

A figure stood by the edge of the pit, tall and cloaked in darkness. His back was to us, but I knew instantly that this was no man. The surrounding air rippled, charged with a malevolence so strong I could barely breathe.

Dev froze, his eyes wide with recognition. This figure—this thing—was something he had seen before, in his dreams, in the nightmares that had haunted him since we set foot on this cursed path.

The figure turned slowly, his movements precise, unnatural. When his face came into view, I felt my blood run cold. His eyes were hollow, dark pits that seemed to swallow the light. And his mouth... twisted into a smile that dripped with malice.

"You know me, Devendran," the figure said, his voice a low, guttural rasp. "I have been with you from the beginning."

Dev took a step back, the amulet clutched tightly in his hand, its warmth now a searing heat. "What do you want?" he asked, his voice tight with barely controlled fear.

The figure's smile widened. "I want what has always been mine. You. Your bloodline. You are the last piece of this curse, Devendran. The end of it begins with you."

Dev's hand shook as he raised the amulet, the glow intensifying. "You can't control me. I won't be your pawn."

The figure chuckled, a sound like bones grinding together. "You think you have a choice? The sins of your ancestors cannot be undone. You are bound to this fate, as they were. There is no escape."

I watched, frozen in place, as Dev's face twisted with anger and fear. I wanted to scream, to pull him away from the edge of that pit, but I couldn't move. The air was heavy, suffocating.

Dev stepped closer to the pit, his jaw clenched. "If you want me, come and take me."

The figure's smile faded, replaced by something darker, more dangerous. "Very well," he hissed.

Dev's grip tightened on the amulet, its light flaring brighter than before. He took a step forward, toward the pit, his heart pounding in his chest. The figure loomed over him, his presence overwhelming.

As Dev stepped to the edge, the ground beneath him trembled. The pit yawned wider, and for a moment, I thought I saw something moving within the mist—something ancient and terrible, waiting to claim him.

But Dev didn't hesitate. He leaped into the abyss, the amulet's light blazing as he disappeared into the darkness.

I screamed his name, but the sound was swallowed by the void.

Dev was gone.

XVII
The Hollow Echoes

I watched, frozen in horror, as Dev disappeared into the abyss. His figure shrank, swallowed by the oppressive darkness that seemed to grow heavier the deeper he fell. It felt like the void itself had claimed him, sealing his fate alongside the curse we had uncovered. My muscles locked with the realization that he was gone. The curse had demanded its price, and it had taken him.

I leaned over the edge, searching the pit below for any sign of him. But there was nothing—no sound, no movement. Just blackness, thicker and more suffocating than the night. My heart pounded in my ears, a frantic rhythm that felt out of place in the stillness that surrounded me.

"Dev..." I whispered, though I knew he couldn't hear me. My voice felt small, swallowed by the abyss.

The faceless entity's words echoed in my mind. "By blood. The pact must be fulfilled by blood." Had Dev's sacrifice freed us from the curse, or had it simply claimed another soul, leaving me alone to face the next step in its unrelenting hunger?

A sharp crack echoed through the cavern, pulling me upright. The stillness broke. Shadows shifted on the walls, grotesque shapes twisting and merging, like phantoms emerging from the stone itself. My breath caught, the air thick with something malevolent.

"Ramesh…"

The voice, soft and unnervingly familiar, slid through the cavern. It was Dev's voice, but something in it was wrong. I whipped around, searching for the source, but there was nothing—only the shadows taunting me.

"Ramesh…"

It was closer now. My heart hammered, my throat tightening with dread. I pressed myself against the jagged rock behind me, my body trembling.

"Dev?" I called out, my voice shaking. But it was met with only silence, the sound of my voice mocking me.

The cavern shifted, shadows rippling like a dark tide closing in around me. I dug my fingers into the rock, as if I could hold on to some semblance of control. But I couldn't. There was no escape. The ground beneath me felt alive, like it was breathing, waiting.

Then I felt it—an icy breath on the back of my neck. Every instinct screamed for me to run, but I couldn't. Slowly, fearfully, I turned.

Dev stood several paces away, his form barely illuminated by the dim light. But something was terribly wrong. His face was a mask, pale and expressionless, eyes vacant, as though he wasn't really there. His clothes, torn and dirt-streaked, clung to his body like a second skin, but the man I knew was gone.

"Dev?" I whispered, unable to believe what I was seeing. "You're alive?"

A thin smile spread across his lips, but it was hollow. His eyes—those lifeless eyes—stared through me.

"I need you to come with me," he said, his voice eerily calm, yet layered with an echo that chilled me to the bone.

I backed away, pressing myself further against the wall. This wasn't Dev. It couldn't be. "What happened to you?"

"I fulfilled the pact," he said, taking a step forward. His movements were slow, deliberate, as if he was fighting against something unseen. With each step, the ground beneath us trembled, a low rumble that seemed to come from the earth itself. "But it's not over. Come with me. I can't hold it back... for long."

I could see it now—the struggle within him. Something dark had taken hold, something far beyond our understanding. The abyss hadn't just taken Dev; it had twisted him, warped him into something unrecognizable.

"Dev, no," I whispered, my voice cracking with fear. "I can't... I won't."

Dev's face contorted, his body shuddering as though something inside him was tearing apart. His hands flew to his head, gripping his skull as a low growl escaped his lips.

"Ramesh... you don't understand," he gasped, his voice cracking with pain. "If you don't... it'll take me... it'll take you too."

The air thickened, the darkness pressing in on us both. The walls of the cavern trembled, and I could feel the ground shift beneath my feet. Dev's form wavered, his body convulsing as if something was trying to tear its way out of him.

And then he lifted his head again, his eyes black as the void. A cold, hollow gaze that wasn't his own stared back at me. I felt my body seize with terror.

"Ramesh!!" His voice, now a desperate roar, shattered the air.

I fumbled for the amulet around my neck, my fingers trembling as they closed around the worn beads. It was all I had left, the only protection against the darkness that surrounded us. I squeezed it hard, feeling a sharp sting as the wood pressed into my palm.

For a moment, the suffocating darkness seemed to pause, hesitating. Dev's body stilled, his vacant eyes flickering, as if the real Dev was fighting to come back. But the shadows twisted around him, pulling him deeper into their grasp.

The ground beneath Dev split open, a jagged crevice widening beneath his feet. The cavern groaned, stones tumbling around us as the earth itself seemed to open up, ready to swallow him whole.

"Dev!" I screamed, lunging toward him.

But it was too late. The ground gave way, and Dev was pulled into the abyss. His last scream echoed through the cavern, his face a twisted mask of terror and confusion, before the darkness consumed him once more.

I found myself trapped as the cavern collapsed. The ancient tomb was falling apart, as though it had completed its purpose, and now it was ready to be buried once again.

I staggered to my feet, my body trembling with exhaustion and grief. The sound of falling stone and the crushing silence that followed weighed heavily on my chest. Dev was gone, and with him, the last hope of breaking the curse.

But as I turned to leave, a faint light flickered in the distance. A glimmer of hope, or perhaps a cruel trick of the mind. I didn't know. But I had no choice—I had to follow it.

With every step, the weight of what had just happened pressed down on me. The curse, the sacrifice, Dev's ultimate moments—it was too much to process. But I couldn't stop. I had to keep moving.

As I stumbled through the narrow tunnel, my breath ragged and shallow, the light grew brighter. I followed it, desperate for any sign of escape, of freedom from the darkness that threatened to consume me.

The tunnel opened up, revealing a narrow shaft of light above. Rainwater trickled down the walls, and the cool air filled my lungs, sharp and refreshing after the suffocating darkness of the cavern.

I climbed, my hands raw and bleeding as I pulled myself up. Every muscle ached, but I couldn't stop. Not now. Not after everything.

When I finally emerged into the open air, I collapsed onto the wet ground; the rain soaking my skin, mixing with the dirt and blood. I lay there, staring up at the stormy sky, the distant roll of thunder echoing in my ears.

But even as I breathed in the cold, fresh air, I knew it wasn't over.

The curse wasn't gone. It hadn't ended with Dev's sacrifice. It was still there, lurking in the shadows, waiting for its next victim.

And I was the only one left.

XVIII
The Abyss Within

The sky was a fractured grey, dawn breaking like a cracked porcelain cup. Thin rays pushed through the stubborn fog, barely illuminating the ground. I stood at the edge of the ancient cavern, its jagged maw yawning beneath me, waiting. The surrounding silence was thick, as though the world itself was holding its breath, anticipating what was to come.

Dust and smoke still clung to the air, settling over the wreckage like a burial shroud. The once-vibrant landscape of Wayanad, ravaged by nature and the supernatural, lay in ruins. Trees, skeletal and charred, stood twisted, their limbs reaching to the sky like they were pleading for something that would never come.

I couldn't stop thinking about him—Dev, my brother, twisted into something unrecognizable. His sacrifice had been in vain, and now I was left to finish what he had started. The curse, insatiable and vicious, demanded more.

Fear didn't grip me like it used to. I had moved beyond it. What boiled inside me now was rage—rage at the centuries-old terror that had torn my family apart. But I couldn't let that anger cloud my mind. I needed to think clearly. I needed to end this.

The ground trembled beneath me. I looked down at the torn earth, freshly ripped open from the collapse. It wasn't just settling—it was alive, moving with a purpose. A pulse, a rhythm. Something was waking beneath the surface. My heart raced as I realized what it was—something was coming.

The earth quaked again, and this time the pulse grew louder. It wasn't just the land moving; it was something deeper, something alive. Despite my desire to escape, I couldn't run away from that immense fissure. I had to see it. I had to know what was waiting for me.

The air around the rocks shimmered, and then, suddenly, the ground split open, widening into a deep fissure. The air that poured out was thick, suffocating, and reeked of decay and something far worse—old blood.

I tightened my grip on the torch I had fashioned from the remnants of the temple. The flame sputtered to life, casting flickering shadows on the walls as I descended into the abyss. The cavern walls pulsed, etched with symbols that would drive anyone mad if they stared too long. Each step felt heavier than the last, as if the very air pressed down on me, whispering things in fractured tongues.

The deeper I went, the more the ground trembled beneath my feet. It was like walking through a cathedral of horrors. The walls seemed to close in on me, and the rhythmic pulse grew louder, almost soothing. I hated it.

Ahead, the tunnel opened into a vast underground chamber. The torch barely lit the edges, but I saw enough. At the center stood an altar, grotesque and slick with blood—centuries of sacrifice etched into its surface. And on that altar, lying unnaturally still, was Dev. Or what was left of him?

My breath caught in my throat as I stared at his twisted body, my fingers trembling around the torch. His face—or the thing that had once been his face—was hollow, eyes empty sockets that seemed to stare straight into the void.

And then he moved. A soft, gurgling sound filled the chamber, an unnatural noise that made my skin crawl. Dev—or whatever had taken his form—stirred, his body jerking upright like a puppet on invisible strings. His gaze met mine, and I saw it—recognition, twisted and broken by whatever had claimed him.

A low, rasping voice echoed through the chamber, vibrating through the walls and into my bones. "Join me, Ramesh... the pact is not yet fulfilled... the curse demands more."

My heart raced, terror gripping me as I stepped back, nearly tripping over the uneven ground. This wasn't Dev anymore. It was something else—a vessel for the curse, a thing of shadows and pain. I could hear it in his voice, not just one voice, but many. Countless souls devoured by the curse over generations. They were all speaking through him, commanding me to submit.

"I... I won't," I stammered, my voice cracking. "This ends here... whether or not you were my brother."

The figure on the altar let out a laugh—a ghastly, distorted sound that shook the chamber. The curse didn't care about my threats. Nothing mattered to it. It only wanted more blood, more souls. It had been feeding for centuries, and it would not stop now.

"No end... only continuation... submission..." The voice oozed through the darkness, thick and liquid, like it was drowning in despair.

The curse was older than us, older than the land itself. It wasn't something that could be fought or reasoned with. It was woven into everything. I could resist, but I knew it would claim me, eventually. It always did.

I clenched the crude blade in my hand, feeling the weight of it. This was my curse now. I had come back knowing I might not survive, but I would not let it win without a fight. I had to sever the bond, break the cycle, or it would just keep going.

Dev's voice twisted again, pleading, threatening, a thousand voices all saying the same thing. The curse had to be completed. It demanded blood, and if I didn't give it willingly, it would take it by force.

But I would not give it anything.

I took a step forward, dipping my blade into the oil on my torch, watching as the flame caught the edge. The figure that had once been Dev stood, watching me, waiting. I knew what I had to do.

The symbols around the altar glowed faintly in the firelight. They were the key. The spiral, the ancient markings—they were what gave the curse its power. If I could destroy them, I could break the curse.

With a quick, precise motion, I flung the torch toward the nearest symbol. Flame leaped across the surface, catching on the ancient carvings. The room trembled as the curse fought back, the power of the symbols weakening under the heat.

Dev's body convulsed, the shadows twisting around him, writhing as if trying to break free. His voice, layered with a thousand others, screamed in agony. The curse was breaking.

The altar cracked, the ancient stone splitting under the pressure of the ritual. I watched as Dev's form crumbled, his body dissolving into ash, swept away into the void.

It was over.

The chamber fell silent, the oppressive weight lifting as the curse faded into nothingness. But as I stood there, surrounded by the remains of the altar, I knew it wasn't truly gone. The curse had been broken, but it wasn't finished with me.

I turned and walked toward the exit, my body heavy with exhaustion. As I stepped into the light of dawn, the weight of what I had done pressed down on me. The curse was broken, but its legacy remained.

XIX

The Watershed

I stood at the edge of the forest, staring out at the burial site, the wind brushing against the blades of grass as if they whispered secrets meant only for me. The morning was eerily still, the silence that lingers after something has ended. It wasn't just the rustling leaves or the cool breeze that stroked my face—it was the feeling of an unspoken farewell. Maybe the souls buried deep beneath the forest were saying their goodbyes, letting me know it was over. Or maybe it was just me, trying to believe that everything had ended.

I turned back toward Aadhira's house, my steps slow. Every inch of ground felt like it pulled at me, like the earth itself was holding on to the memory of what had happened down in that forsaken chamber. The house emerged from the mist as I approached, unchanged by the horrors it had sheltered. The vibrant bougainvillaea still spilled over the veranda, the lawn was still neatly trimmed, as if none of it had been touched by the supernatural chaos that had unfolded in the past few days. Every brick, every worn tile, felt like an extension of Aadhira herself—her sanctuary, her home.

Crossing the threshold, I was hit with the familiarity of it all. The creaking wood beneath my feet, the scent of tea that seemed to linger in the air despite no one having brewed it for days. Everything about the place felt welcoming, heartbreakingly human, in a way that almost made me forget the horrors outside. But the silence was different today. It wasn't just the quiet of an empty house—it was the stillness of a place that knew something had changed. Something final.

I made my way through the hallway, my fingers trailing along the walls as if the worn paint could anchor me back to reality. My mind was still racing with everything that had happened—the visions, the dark force that had swallowed Dev. His voice echoed in my head, not as the tortured cries I'd heard in that chamber, but as the laughter I'd grown up with, now lost in the darkness.

This would be my last time here. I knew it deep down. The house held too many memories, too many ghosts. But before I left, I had one last thing to do. One last task.

I headed to Aadhira's study, where the laptop sat waiting on the small oak table. Everything we had gathered—every piece of evidence that tied Ravi Verma to his crimes—was stored there. All the documents, the photographs, the testimonies. It was all ready. All I had to do was send it to Suresh, the one man with enough power and determination to bring Ravi to justice.

The screen flickered to life as I opened the laptop, its glow casting a faint light in the dim room. I began drafting the email to Suresh, attaching the massive file of evidence that Aadhira had compiled. My fingers moved mechanically, typing out the facts, summarizing the discoveries. But my mind was elsewhere—numb, detached, like I was watching someone else do the work. The urgency I had felt in the beginning had long since faded. All that was left now was a cold, obvious sense of duty.

I wasn't doing this just for Aadhira. I was doing it for Dev, too. For his soul, twisted and consumed by the darkness, but still there, still fighting. I owed it to him.

My hand hovered over the "Send" button. For a moment, I hesitated. A tremor of doubt crept in, the weight of everything crashing down on me.

"I'll do this for you, Dev... for you, Aadhira," I whispered into the silence, my voice barely above a breath.

And then, I clicked "Send."

There was no significant shift, no sudden feeling of release or resolution. The email simply left, carried through invisible wires and signals, making its way to Suresh's desk. He would take it from here. He had the power to shine a light on Ravi Verma's crimes, to make sure the truth was known. Once the public saw the evidence, there would be no escape from Verma.

Justice was inevitable now. It had to be.

I closed the laptop, the weight of it sinking into the table as though it carried the last of my energy with it. The house seemed to sigh, as if it too understood that this was the end. Aadhira's spirit was no longer here—she had moved on, finding peace in knowing that her story would be told. And Dev... his fate was more complicated. But I believed, somehow, that he had found his own kind of redemption.

I stood, letting the silence of the house settle over me one last time. Then, without looking back, I left Aadhira's home, leaving behind the ghosts and the memories that would forever haunt its walls.

News spread quickly in Kerala. Once Suresh received the files, he wasted no time releasing them to every corner of India's media network. Journalists dove into the scandal with zeal, unearthing the dark truth Ravi Verma had worked so hard to bury. The evidence—the same files Ravi believed he'd hidden beneath landslides and corpses—now flashed on screens across the country, from New Delhi to Vadodara.

Within days, the scandal exploded. Ravi, once hailed as a visionary for transforming barren lands into thriving communities, was now exposed. The media peeled back the layers of his empire, revealing a man fueled by greed and carelessness, indifferent to the devastation he had caused. Grief and anger washed over the nation as families whose homes stood on cursed ground came forward. The media splashed images of broken homes and the grieving loved ones of those buried beneath them, trapped by the very foundations that sheltered them.

Kerala, especially, seethed with fury. For too long, people had been afraid to speak out against the likes of Ravi Verma. But now, they gathered in crowds outside his mansion, their voices unified in one demand: justice. The once untouchable businessman was now a pariah, his name whispered in disgust across the state and beyond.

The case could no longer be ignored. The scale of Ravi's deceit and corruption became a national issue. Investigators combed through the evidence and found a damning trail. From fraudulent land deals to reckless construction projects, Ravi had built his empire on the bones of the land. He had ignored warnings, bypassed safety protocols, and silenced anyone who questioned his methods. Entire neighborhoods were buried because of his greed.

The law moved swiftly, freezing Ravi's assets—his luxury homes, his stock holdings, everything tied to his tainted empire. But Ravi, ever the strategist, tried to flee, hoping to escape the storm he had unleashed. It wasn't long before the authorities caught up with him. He was arrested at Trivandrum International Airport, handcuffed, and escorted by officers through the flashing lights of news cameras. Journalists hurled questions, but Ravi kept his head down, muttering to himself, refusing to acknowledge the chaos he had created.

The court wasted no time, and soon, a trial date was set. The entire nation watched as the judiciary, feeling the pressure of public outrage, took an uncompromising stance. No leniency would be shown. Every piece of evidence was scrutinized—each document, each testimony, each piece of the puzzle that painted Ravi Verma not as a victim of circumstance but as the architect of an entire region's suffering.

I sat in the back of the courtroom during those sessions, watching as Ravi faced the consequences of his actions. He looked like a different man—a far cry from the smug, untouchable figure I had once despised. His empire had crumbled, and with it, so had his arrogance. The trial dragged on, with each day revealing more of the rot that had festered beneath the surface of his business dealings. It should have felt like victory, like justice, but it felt empty. Aadhira was gone. The people who had perished, lost in the landslide or ruined by his decisions, were still dead. Nothing could bring them back.

The gavel finally came down, sentencing Ravi to decades behind bars. His assets were seized, his properties repossessed, his empire dismantled piece by piece. Justice, it seemed, had caught up with him, though it felt far too late. For the families who had suffered, for Aadhira, for Dev—there was no real reparation.

Even as the court ruled against him, Ravi's eyes held no remorse. Only a hollow emptiness. He had lost everything, yet it was the weight of his shattered pride that had broken him. The man who had once been untouchable now stood as a cautionary tale—a symbol of what happens when greed consumes.

When the sentencing ended, I walked out of the courtroom, the sun blinding as it hit my face. People around me murmured, some in relief, others in grief. But I felt neither. Justice had come, yes, but it had arrived too late for so many. Ravi would rot in prison, but what about the lives he had ruined? What about the stories that would never be told, the futures that had been stolen?

And yet, there was something. Aadhira had hoped for this—had fought for this. The land would be returned to its rightful owners, taken out of the grip of corporate greed. The industrial chains that had bound it would be broken, and perhaps, just perhaps, the land itself could heal.

It wasn't the victory I had envisioned. It wasn't the justice I had wanted for Aadhira or Dev. But it was something. And sometimes, that had to be enough.

As I stood there, staring out at the courthouse steps, I whispered under my breath, "For you, Aadhira. For you, Dev."

And with that, I walked away, the weight of everything still pressing against my chest, but lighter somehow. Justice had come. Now it was time for healing.

✺

As the summer faded, and with Ravi Verma finally rotting in prison, the hills of Wayanad found an uneasy calm. Word spread quickly—locals whispered of a government campaign, in partnership with environmentalists, that would restore the villages buried beneath Ravi's destruction. They called it Moksha. It was more than just reparations—it was a plea to the ancient gods, a way to seek forgiveness for the sins committed against this sacred land. The people believed the gods, in their righteous fury, had caused the devastation.

The heart of this movement was an environmental ordinance, aimed at reclaiming the desecrated earth. Ravi's industrial scars would be erased, and the land would be reborn, transformed into a protected ecological reserve. It would become a forest once more, as it had been before greed tore through it. This time, human hands would tend to it with reverence, each step taken with a quiet understanding of what had been lost.

But healing the land wasn't enough. The dead needed peace, too. And that's where I came in.

I had joined the villagers, standing beside them as they started rituals in order to honour the spirits and release them from the pain that had held them captive for so long. A pandit, an ancient high priest revered for his wisdom, was summoned. He wasn't there out of duty alone—he felt the weight of the souls trapped in this place, and he offered them the peace they had waited decades to receive.

The first day of the rituals was heavy with anticipation. Villagers, officials, and spiritual leaders gathered at the river, the same river that had witnessed tragedy after tragedy. Now, it had become something else—a symbol of cleansing, of washing away the sorrow that had poisoned this place.

The rituals spanned days, each chant, each offering carrying the weight of generations. But the final rite—it was for the trapped souls, the ones Aadhira had fought for, even after death. Aadhira's name was whispered like a prayer now. Her story had become a legend, a tale of a woman who had given everything for justice. The truth and myth blurred together, but it didn't matter. The people remembered her, and that was enough.

As the sun dipped below the horizon, the pandit stood at the burial site, where I had once stood with Aadhira and Dev. His voice rose, chanting in the ancient tongue, calling on the gods to free the spirits bound to the land. The words echoed through the still air, lifting toward the twilight sky. I stood there, breathless, feeling the weight of the moment pressing down on me.

I watched as the chants seemed to ripple through the air, the weight of generations lifting with each word. The forest hushed, the river—always roaring—fell silent, as if it too was holding its breath. It felt like the world was watching, waiting. And then, as the last words were spoken, something shifted. The air lightened, the tension that had suffused the land for so long dissolved. Peace settled over the hills, quiet but undeniable.

The rituals ended, but none of us moved. We stood there, bathed in moonlight, the sky parting just enough to let it wash over us. I stayed where I was; the others drifting away, but I couldn't leave just yet. I felt something—something only I could sense. The veil between the living and the dead had thinned, just for a moment. It was then that I felt it—a hand, warm and familiar, resting on my shoulder. *I didn't turn. I didn't need to. I knew it was him.*

"When you're ready," I whispered, my voice cracking in the stillness. "I hope you'll find peace too."

The wind whispered through the trees, soft and comforting, and for the first time in what felt like forever, the world was still.

⁝

It became my weekly ritual—returning to the memorial site where a simple granite marker stood for those buried by the landslide of 2024. The stone was nothing extravagant, just a boulder smoothed by years of rain, with a small plaque in Malayalam:

"In Memory of Those Lost and Forgotten."

Beneath that boulder rested the remains of those who could finally find peace. After the last rituals were complete, the excavation team had done the sacred work of retrieving the bodies trapped in the earth, carefully interring them with the dignity they deserved. Families had been notified, permits granted, and a promise made—this would be their final resting place, untouched by greed or malice. This land would be theirs forever.

I would sit by the stone, feeling the earth beneath me, the trees that now grew strong in the soil once so ravaged by destruction. Nature had reclaimed its rightful place, the forest slowly returning to its former glory. The flora they planted had taken root, breathing new life into the land. And with it, a strange sense of calm settled over me.

This was where I found my peace. I wasn't alone, not really. The birds sang in the branches above, monkeys chattered in the distance, and bees hummed, going about their work. The supernatural terror that had haunted me for so long—the visions that had clawed at my mind—was finally fading. What remained in its place was quieter, gentler. The sunset's soft, golden light would filter through the trees, and in those moments, I felt something close to healing.

I liked to believe that somewhere, Aadhira had found her peace too. She wasn't beneath the ground here, not her—she was somewhere else, somewhere far beyond this world. She had done her part, uncovering the truth that set those souls free, that freed me, too. The guilt, the anger, the doubt—all those dark parts of me I could never seem to escape—had loosened their grip.

Sitting there on the ground, I wasn't just mourning those who had died with the landslide. I was mourning the man I had been, the one who had carried all that weight for so long. The man who had been burdened by a past he couldn't outrun.

But now, there was a stillness inside me. It wasn't happiness, but it was something better—a fragile peace, fragile but real. And as I sat there, watching the day fade, I felt ready for whatever came next.

Months drifted by, like the slow turning of pages in an old, dog-eared novel. After the court's ruling, Ravi Verma's empire crumbled. His stolen wealth was returned to the people he had wronged—families who had suffered, finally seeing justice, a justice that was swift and, for once, relentless.

The rumours about the landslide site being haunted lingered in the air for a while longer. But strangely, no harm came to those who ventured near. The stories changed—tales of terror became whispers of reconciliation. The spirits, once angry and restless, now seemed at peace. They weren't malevolent anymore; they had become silent guardians, watching over the land and those who lived nearby. It was as if the land itself, scarred by history, had made peace with its past.

Kerala felt quieter now, more settled. The ghosts of men who once wielded unchecked power had receded, just as the ghosts of the land had. Aadhira's name, though, had taken on a life of its own. It wasn't spoken in fear anymore. Her name had become something sacred, an anthem for the forgotten. People whispered it when they prayed near the landslide site—not out of dread, but with reverence, as though her spirit was woven back into the land itself, a reminder of the price paid to bring truth to light.

In time, I knew it was my turn to leave Wayanad. There was nothing left for me here, not anymore. The call of somewhere new—somewhere far from the memories of these shadowed hills—had grown louder. I packed lightly, taking only what I needed. A journal came with me, its pages filled with thoughts, reflections, and the weight of what had happened. To some, the words might seem sad, full of loss. But to me, something else had grown between those lines—something like hope, or maybe something bigger, something I couldn't quite name yet.

As I walked away from those hills, no ghosts followed. No voices murmured in my ear. I left the house behind, not as a tragic memory, but as something that had simply reached its end. There was a strange finality in it, not heavy or bitter, but peaceful. I had accepted that not everything needed to be carried forward. Some things—some burdens, some memories—are laid to rest.

The road ahead stretched out before me, bathed in sunlight. It was untouched, serene, waiting.

I wasn't the man who had first arrived in Wayanad—haunted by curses, weighed down by the shadows of a brother lost too soon. That version of me was gone, left behind with the rest. I walked forward now, just another soul among millions, moving toward the light,

ready for whatever the next chapter had in store.
And for the first time in a long time, I was at peace.

www.ingramcontent.com/pod-product-compliance
Lightning Source LLC
Chambersburg PA
CBHW031624170726
47990CB00017B/366